The Ormering Tide
Kathryn Williams

The Ormering Tide
Kathryn Williams

ISBN 978-1-903110-76-8

First published in this edition 2020 by Wrecking Ball Press.

Book design by humandesign.co.uk

Supported using public funding by
**ARTS COUNCIL
ENGLAND**

Acknowledgements

Early on when writing The Ormering Tide, riddled with imposter syndrome and fear, I got support and great advice from Jacob Polley, Kirsty Logan and Laura Barnett, all amazing writers who never talked down to me, only encouraged.

I have been lucky in finding Kirsty McLachlan, my agent at Morgan Green Creatives, and Wrecking Ball Press as a home for the book. Thanks and love to Mum and Dad, Neil Le Flohic, Polly Paulusma, Chris Collins, Becca, Sara, Tom McRae, Tim Lott, Rosa Rankin Gee, Nev Clay, Kath Kenny and Emma Latham who took the time to read early versions and gave me gentle but truthful support.

Kathryn Williams

Ormers, also known as ear shells, are abalones that live on the lower shores of the Channel Islands. They can only be accessed to harvest on the big spring tides.

You may only catch ormers on the day of the new or full moon, and then two days after that.

They use a foot (like a limpet) to cling and attach themselves to the seabed.

People go out and turn over rocks and boulders to find them, which is remarkably difficult thanks to the natural camouflage of their outer shell.

They can live for more than fifteen years.

Inside ormers hold a mother of pearl, a sandy shining, crisscrossed by rainbows of light.

Its iridescent treasure has been used throughout history in furniture, buttons, musical instruments and jewellery.

Processing the past only ever happens after the fact.

Of course! How could it be any other way?

We walk back into empty rooms and fill what was once there with our minds.

Switch on the lights.

Light the fires.

Adjust the crooked frames.

Paint walls blue that may have been green.

Prologue

The nights I have spent in this room.

The same silence.

I can hear my heart. Not a spurning ache or a yearning pull. Just turning over, waiting to move on.
My body is honest.
The chimney over there, a rib cage. My secrets are all inside it.
My brain has lit itself and wants to float away up through the chimney from smoke to cloud.

I used to spend my time wondering and imagining a different world, making up rules for how things were.
Things grew at night, plants used up every inch of themselves just to break free from winter.

The time to say something passed me, and I was left with words, rolling back and forth in the tides until they were smooth and round and could fit between my tongue and the roof of my mouth, with my jaw shut and a smile on my face.
I lie back on the same pillow and listen to the nothingness.
There is something. Always. Filling the stillness.
The nothing is stuffing dead feathers in a cushion.
Chair legs scraping downstairs, a wooden creak, a foot, a stair being stood on then stood off. The wind hitting the tree and the gate, which still gets left open by the brothers — even though they are old enough to make a gate themselves, never mind shut one.

Tomorrow I will be married. I become 'they'.
'They' were going to the mainland after the ceremony, with the islanders waving and throwing rice into the air. 'They' would think about a new place to live.
Birds will come and eat at the rice until there was no sign we even

stood by the stone steps.

And that will be the end of my life as it is on the common.

Does the world outside change you inside?

If I lived up on the cliff, closer to the sea spray and the sky, would that change me?

Would I grow wings?

I didn't separate Mrs. Bertram from where she was. She is the edge. The cliff and its sea spray. She looks out and down from a window, while I was looking out and up. I only imagined I knew her just like landscapes are emotions we breathe in.

A flat expanse, an easy deep breath, a mountain feels cold in the nose valley, swallowed whole like an oyster. A glassy lake is tipped and drunk right down to the cold icy stone bottom.

We sit inside them, then they are inside us.

I walk to the window to make it real.

The curtain in my hand is soft and I hold the curl of it and pull it down to stroke it to the inside of my palm. It catches slightly on a rough piece of skin, just a fraction. The rest is a smooth sensation that I repeat in little circles as I look past my own reflection in the glass. At night the earth rises up in its darkness. It always has, it always will. Its breath up and into the dark night. The common, the back of a furry fern beast, flattening out around the cottage, like it's been hit with the back of a shovel. It keeps the dark memory of Mr. Willow in the dark house over there.

I wonder if Mrs. Bertram looks at that square of dark land. From up there, is it any flatter?

Doesn't matter.

He's deadwood and she's up on the cliff out of reach of his bony branches.

The big house was just a cut out silhouette, a black profile portrait. Maman had her mother's face in profile in a gold oval frame near her bed. Her shadow sitting in front of a lamp, side on, sat still while scissors cut her face into the paper. We tried to do the same for Maman when it rained outside and we were young.

But the brothers had tried for only a few minutes before cutting off each other's paper noses, then running out in to the mud and rain.

I'd been happy with the cut that I had made of Maman.

She said, "Well done, Rozel, you tried hard," but there was no recognition of herself.

I had tried hard to capture her, twisting my paper to the will of the scissors, seeing her face fresher for the task of looking and cutting. Cutting her out of a page. Drawing her out. The fall and fail. There is a gap between what we see and want to show, what our hands and eyes can recreate. The frustration of act over thought.

Marriage is like drawing. Would the act and the thought match?

One thing I knew for certain: my thoughts were too much to share. Too fast, too big.

Who would have time to share my daily process without losing their own?

Rolling round, glass marbles in the soft bag. The stories I've made in my own head have become as concrete as any memory outside. I can't separate them from the other books on the shelf.

We are all a library full of fact and fiction.

My heart was beating. I had run down a hill, in my mind. I took my hand away from the curtains and felt it thudding through my jumper.

Thank you, heart, for interrupting. My mind isn't to make the choices, only my heart.

Truth in a heart rings like a bell. There it goes, running down steep hills away from my thoughts. Away from me.

Chapter One

Pops was at the Smugglers Inn. Of course he was.

Before I broke my arm it was morning. We were at the back door. The heat from standing next to this boulder, my mother. She blocked out the cold salty wind coming off the sea. January years, February years.

I was up to her waist, she had her sky blue dress with an apron over the top, cotton on cotton. She was the breakwater rocks. A big brass bell. Her centre of gravity was so strong I couldn't imagine a single thing budging her from that point.

She was shouting. Through the cold air towards the vegetable patch. Cold smoke in long clouds. I heard a click. It was metal. Fingers clicking. Maman stopped shouting. She didn't move. I felt her muscles tense under all that padding.

On the ground was what looked like a dog. The rain was in thin lines stitching a net curtain blowing into our faces. My eyes squinted at the flicks of water.

A dog? A rotting tweed coat? Digging into the frozen ground. With his hands and knuckles, paws red raw. He was thin, as thin as the rain.

Was he a dog?

Was he a man?

He was shouting back at Maman. So weak. It was like air coming out of a balloon. He was crumpling up as the words that sounded like barking came towards us. A small dog barking to leave his bone alone.

Then the noise stopped.

He had found a carrot. He was pulling it from the ground, scrabbling for the edges. The dirt was hard and he was scratching with his nails. Scraping a mud bowl into fingernailed gratings.

An orange icicle, hardly a vegetable at all. It could have been a stone. It would have been a stone against stones of his teeth. I stood a little closer to Maman. Warm cotton wafts, the smells of washing and home.

The finger click had been his gun.

In warning he had cocked it. He lay it down. Looking down at the ground then turning his head on the side towards us and back to the carrot, a hinged gate swinging back and forth. He was sitting in our garden. The mound of earth that he was, huddling to a frozen carrot with his cold gun and his sore hands like it was a piece of gold.

Maman stamped her foot. Angry at the thievery. The ground shook. Her ample jelly hips wobbled then balanced back into position. She hissed shoo, turned and turned me with her back into the cottage.

With not one inch of fear, she turned her back to this man and his gun. Shutting the door behind us both, kicking it closed with the back of her foot. And as if nothing had happened, she walked to the hearth and put the kettle onto its black warm circle like a hammer.

BANG.

The next morning normal things happened.

The sun came up at the left. The cliff was still standing and the sound of gulls laughed at old Mrs. Bertram on her bike pedalling with her knees out to each side. She wavered (as if for the crowd) like a tightrope walker, over the thin part of cliff to her house. It was not for her to gasp. It was for us down below to worry.

There was not enough colour in the world. I missed the yellow of the gorse on the common in winter. The flat and wild expanse of it before the beach. The only two buildings on it were ours and Mr. Willow's surrounded by trees and bushes. It wasn't a kept land, the common. If anything it looked as if it was never combed or even went to the barbers. It was as flat as our table until it got to the edges of the cove where it would meet all the hill and the cliffs. You could see the narrow tracks then, scrawled up the steep cliff edges. In the thick of the common, you could think you were on a pathway, a line as if it had been walked, but find yourself in the middle of a thorny gorse bush with no way to go except backwards. We were the rabbits who knew it better than anyone else in the cove. In winter you could see through the skeletons of the trees and find a way out. The sand would whip up with the wind and hit at our bare legs like little pins. All I wanted was for things to start growing again and winter to stop.

I wiped my face with the cloth that lay on the side of the bowl.

My life was very much like that bowl, filled new each day. The sloshing around of the same faces, the same concave world, filling in and tipping out. Outside the window, I heard a faint sound of the bell of Mrs. Bertram's bike clink on its own as she came over a bump towards the fence and along the lower path, letting it be known she had reached the bottom with unruly bells and squeaking brakes. She was the sound of bulbs pushing up from the ground in spring, the clink of china cups, crisp and bell fresh.

Mrs. Bertram was on the cliff. No safety net today or any other day, teetering on the edge. Watching her almost fall off that cliff. She didn't fall though. She wasn't the one who fell.

Today in the garden, the shovel, left in the frozen soil ready to dig when it had softened up. You see even fewer people in winter; they are waiting for the island to warm up, just like our shovel. Where we live is so small most of the faces on the island you know: either they come from families that all look alike and you can trace that nose to a long line of owners going back and passing that same-shaped nose from one another, or you've seen that face before because there aren't enough miles here.

The soldiers had gone from the island only leaving the things that would sink them on a trip home, like our concrete sea wall and the watch tower and the underground places like the hospital that they closed off because of all the sadness that was seeping out. There were ones who didn't leave and ones who said they would come back. Many other men came later looking for work after the war. Islanders still remembered being occupied and kept themselves to themselves, distrusting that these non-islanders wouldn't take from them again. There was no more war but there were still sides.

I was small then, only remembered the dog in the garden. But the adults talked of strangers in the same way as they talked of the soldiers. The memory was still fresh enough to put them all in the same box.

Strangers were rare to me. Most who came over for work never ventured as far as our cove. They worked in the kitchens of hotels or picked in the fruit farms on the east side. For how small our island was, people didn't move much. You could hear a main town accent and how it differs to our small cove.

Maman was always correcting me: "Rozel, it's stranger," when I would shout, "soldier."

The garden that winter, the stranger, the soldier. That's all I can remember of soldiers, and Maman and Pops don't talk about them. Pops doesn't say much of anything. I don't know now if it was a soldier or a stranger or a dog. I remember. I forget. Then remembering gets lost in hanging lines of mist, they cloud the common in the coldest winter, I retrace my memory but I am never in the same time, inside it or out looking in.

Chapter Two

Over winter my trips to the well had been the worst job. The steps down to the water were slippery and cold and if I put my hand on the wall to steady myself the edges would bite at me in sharp anger.

The water didn't want to be taken, and the bucket would slosh on the walk back to the cottage and burn its coldness through my dress and redden my skin. I would come and sit to dry the patches out by the stove and watch the steam rise up and out.

Maman calls steam 'ghost water'.

Ice was ghostly too. And what was water? Hiding in all those three forms. The changeling. What did water do at night?

Maman and the brothers would often laugh at my questions. Even if they were laughing at my expense I would love to watch them flop forward, helpless with the contagion. Pops would tip his head forward, silent as ever, and look at me from the top of his eyes and I would try to keep most of what I thought to myself.

Spring was spreading through the trees and widening our world again. We could go further from the cottage, the brothers always further than me, and soon we would have our common and its twisting ways to play in again.

That morning, I had gone to the well, the crisp patterned frost on all the leaves, all around the edges as if someone had delicately dipped it in crystal sugar. I couldn't help trying a taste of them in case the sweetness was true. Cold and green was all I could taste.

I was almost out of the shadow from the cliff, another twenty steps and I would feel the sun on my back. I was swinging the bucket and it was squeaking but only every third or fourth swing. And I was trying to guess when it would make a sound. So I wasn't really concentrating when I tripped. My arm hit the edge of the bucket and the pain was sharp.

I looked back to see what I had tripped on. A log.

A leg.

Turning I saw the foot in an L shape up towards a body that had balled itself up. I recognised the brown rough material and the boots with no laces. My arm was throbbing and the pain felt hot. I leaned over him.

What was I expecting? Wake him up? To get a closer look while I could. He was a pale blue. He had the same little sugar frosting around his eyes as the leaves further back had had. I touched him with my foot to wake him but he didn't budge. I could see the sun line on the ground coming ever so slowly towards us as the sun was lifting itself over the back of the cliff. When the sun came, would he thaw and wake and yawn like the picture of the flowers and trees in my seasons book?

I felt my body go forward and back, forward and back. Should I carry on with the water bucket or go back to the cottage?

I'd go that bit further and get the water and tell when I got home.

I kept looking behind me, feeling I would see him following me. Every few steps I heard his footsteps limping behind me, but it was my steps. I got to the well. And when I swapped the bucket from one hand to the other, I realised my arm was throbbing and weak. I leaned in and got just over half full. Then turned back and up.

All I could hear as I walked back towards the cottage was the squeak of the swing of the bucket. Every three times and then for no reason it wouldn't squeak. Just my breathing, the bucket squeak, the small slosh of the water, the blood pulsing in my ears and the hot in my arm. As I approached him, he was still and unmoved, though now the sun was on him and the cliff line had reached his boot.

I stepped over his leg, expecting it to kick. The pulse in my ears ran as I ran til I got back.

I walked through the door into the kitchen, smelling breakfast and the heat of the stove hitting me straight in the face, I felt myself sink towards the floor and I felt a black come from the sides of my eyes.

Maman's hands had grabbed me and put me on a chair.

"What is wrong?" she asked. It felt like far away.

"My arm," I said. "I tripped."

"Let's look."

She felt along it and I felt the snap and pain. The room swung again. She couldn't be sure but it looked broken. Maman was talking to Pops quietly.

"We need to get you to the doctor," Pops said, resting my face in his big rough hand.

I tipped my head back. The ceiling swung to and fro, a slapping sea inside my head sloshed and swished and I closed my eyes and dug into the help.

The time had gone for saying any more and I just couldn't get a break from all the talking to tell them about the man with the sugar frosted eyes.

Later at the doctor's when asked what I had fallen on, my mouth wouldn't say. Would it seem stranger to not have mentioned the man, in the kitchen? I looked from face to face, feeling guilty. What if the sun had reached him and thawed him enough to bring life into him, if only for a few minutes?

I just shrugged. It hurt.

Sitting in the waiting room. In the hush of time ticking. The chairs of plastic leather and metal with no space for movement. Everyone whispered or stepped lightly as if a baby were sleeping. But there was no baby, nothing but a noise coming from a heater that clipped the cold out of the air and pushed the disinfectant smells up our noses. Maman was fidgeting with a loose piece of cotton on her dress. Barely managing to grasp it in her thick work fingers. She was attempting to knot it but kept slipping because of the slightly too small length, beginning again around her finger with a tut.

The postman was delivering a parcel to the reception hatch.

He leaned in saying, "Aye aye!"

The receptionist put her finger to her lips, slowly lifted her head up from the desk, shifted back a little. *There will be no joy in here*, she seemed to say with her eyes.

He leaned back out of the hatch, but like a dog whose tail was beyond them for wagging, his foot was tapping to some song in his head.

He whispered, "Have you heard? They found a man on the

common. Froze himself to death." He scratched his head as means of an exclamation. "The one bleeding time there is a frost on the island and he sleeps out."

Maman looked up. Everyone had heard the news. My stomach felt full of stones.

For the first time I could feel the pain of him in my arm. Dead bodies turn hard as stone to break bones.

I wouldn't need to tell now.

And my story sat inside with the stone in my stomach and the break in my bone. A hairline fracture, a crack in the ice, a growing frost up along a strand of grass.

I would see him stand up behind me in my dreams, inside my head, on the pillow, walking towards me, the bucket would swing and squeak and I would run and slip til waking hot and panicked, throwing the pillow at the wall hoping he was taken with it.

An untouched world the secret in me, a small cave where I thought I had the capacity to hide more.

As I grew the years itched and knitted away the broken bone, weaving ivy over the secret of that day. I stopped searching for my own, looking for other people's, seeing if they let slip something I could keep. Soft inside shells. Ear shells.

Chapter 3

Things did start growing. First little jabs of green came up around the edges of the vegetable squares. Little knives of defiance. They had pushed a fair way up through the brown clagging soil. Determined to break through and wish themselves flowers.

They grew every time I forgot to look and then white snowdrops hung their heads down like shy child brides.

They looked at the ground contemplating how they came above the brown mass of all that had passed.

My brothers would give them a sly kick as they went past that made my stomach turn and twist. They would walk past the bushes by the wood hut and just mindlessly pull at leaves to feel the snap and then sprinkle them the way they had been. My poor plants. All that time becoming something, then out of boredom pulled and gone.

I sat back on the grass rubbing my hands softly each side of me. Combing and stroking the grass this way, then the other. I was the sea, breathing up and down and I lay back imagining the clouds as the bottom of boats casting shadows on me down here. Down at the bottom of the sea. The engine of the clouds drifting and their passing over put maps on the back of my eyelids. I was holding them up. I was the sea and it was my choice that they stayed on the surface. I felt all the blood rushing into my face. I was feeling power inside me. The feelings leaders or teachers feel.

I got up.

I ran into the kitchen and straight into the side of Maman. I was hitting higher on her. Her waist had become a lower horizon and I was moving closer towards her face.

Maman felt my growing too. She was wishing shoes could stretch. She would talk these thoughts into her soup like salt and Pops would nod over at the table like the slow chop of carrots. Pops and his weathered face. My brown school satchel gave more away than that face of his. It hardly moved. His head would nod, and turn and look, but his face could stay so still, while his eyes would watch from behind the wall, occasionally twinkling at something said.

I would feel myself growing in bed, hear the inches add. One day I tried to see if I could hear grass growing by spending a whole day on the lawn trying to ignore all the other noises around me. I came to the conclusion that things only grow at night and they shrink in the day. When I suggested that to the room, everyone laughed, even Pops, though his was a silent movement of his shoulders.

"Oh, you are funny, spending your thoughts on these things, Rozel."

Maman's words of soft warm velvet, consoling, as she glanced over at Pops who flashed his eyes at her without moving anywhere else, locked on hers and then down at the table.

And that was us in our kitchen in our cottage on the common.

That is us. Our family.

Bunny was a part of the common too. He was always there, an add-on to the brothers three. He lived up on the cliff with his mum, Mrs. Bertram. Bunny's mum never came to the cottage, but Bunny was here knocking to play most days. I opened the door, a cake slice worth of opening, I stood in the V space. He asked if John was there. His "s" was a "th" like he was muting the sound with his tongue. His shoulder twitched upwards after he spoke, his body shoving the words, pushing them out.

I laughed with the joy of it. It was like speaking to an animal. Not like anyone else. Bunny blushed, his eyes fell down then his head. He turned and left.

That was the first time I remember him speaking only to me. I had never laughed at his voice and his way of talking before, even though I'd heard him speak before. When I notice something unusual about someone, I try to pretend that there is nothing different.

I can't stop myself taking an extra sly glance at the man's neck who loads the ferry. His tattoo is only part on show. It's an arm or a claw leading down past his collar. I can't very well ask, "What animal do you have in your shirt?"

Maybe it is an entire zoo and only that poor paw is feeling fresh air. Maman says we are all part on show with the rest guessed.

Bunny must have thought I found him funny because of his lisp but I could listen to him all day. He stops himself talking, I've seen him do it, self-conscious and like Pops, rationing his words, often listening when he could probably add better things into the conversation.

His shell sound speak suited him.

The sea talking.

His hair looked like it had been combed by the sea, coming together in the middle in a soft shallow tuft of a wave. I'd see him, squinting at a horizon line, off into the distance. Was he looking or thinking? Drawn between the end of his gaze and his eyes, wondering if the river was flowing out or in. I closed the door and the kitchen went a little darker.

Now he thought I was just a stupid child that laughs at someone with a lisp.

A soft heartburn as I breathed out.

"Who was that?" asked Maman

"Bunny Bertram," I said.

"That shouldn't even be his name," she said, looking out of the kitchen window and seeing him the other side of our gate, picking off the yellow circles of lichen with his fingernail.

"Bunny? Isn't it short for Brian?"

"No, Bertram."

I looked at the back of him, walking along the other side of our gate and the scratched brown line left in the yellow patch of lichen on the fence post facing the cottage. The yellow under his fingernails taken back up the cliff.

After that, walking to school, or out on the common, Bunny didn't use words on me again. I missed hearing him talk. The whispering licks of wind in dry grass, the circling of dry sand in swirls. The wind at the top of the cliffs rushing past the holes in my ears, all had the same lisp.

The brothers could fill the whole sky with their words, and they did.

Shouting black clouds at each other, back and forth, over the top, overlapping, crashing, thunderous words. There was barely room to breathe. Especially John, shouting his orders in the spring's crisper air, flying at the front of the formation of them, honking geese all the way through to the rising heat of summer. All of them a noise that I wished would be quiet. John leading the way, his foghorn directions and orders barked to anyone who would listen. I don't even know why, but we all did.

Chapter 4

Maman was worrying her thumb across her chin.

The brothers had not been home for such a long time. She didn't know where they were and it was getting towards dusk.

"I can feel something is not quite right tonight," she said, rubbing the sides of her hips as if that was where the feeling was. "I don't know what it is but there's a darkness creeping in faster than the night into this kitchen."

Her fretting started on other things in the kitchen as she spoke, plates were lifted onto their shelves, crumbs brushed with her hand into the other hand and tipped into the sink. She turned and looked at me.

Maman had these moments. Everyone felt it was a bit dramatic, the way she could be. Like an actress had come to play our mother but gone a bit over the top. But it was as real as any other ailment she got. She really felt these things inside her. When bad thoughts happen it was as if she had been struck by lightning or bitten by an animal or cut by a thorn. The bad thoughts got worse this time of year as summer slid into autumn, nights drawing in, her thoughts became longer shadows stretching out fears of dark loss pools.

She had an invisible string to her children, it could let out like a spider's web, turn corners and knot back on itself but if she ever felt it slacken, she knew it would take over, it would cloud her.

Maman's thread had broken a few years before me, when the baby that had been inside her, came out dead. I heard them talking about it, that's how I know. I shouldn't have been listening but I do over and over, seduced by their soft words to each other. Pops' silent way is a road for Maman's words. Maman was always telling us that talking things through tidied a mind. But she shook and her voice trembled that night I listened in. Only with the steady silent road that Pops laid out for her did the words eventually roll out, like her tears. I had tiptoed away hearing her crying, muffled into Pops shoulder. I had gone back to my room and hugged the pillow on my bed. Poor

Maman, my Maman. Her belly was a grave and a garden. Nobody got to see the baby except Maman, Pops, and the doctor.

What do you do with a baby that loses its thread?

They were together for so long, since they were children themselves. Maman and Pops had been sweethearts at school. Maman had always lived in this bit of the island. It was Pops who was an outsider, coming from three miles away. She always said he brought his family's nose and the east wind into her family. She was right. We all had his nose. Long and robust. I always thought our noses looked better on the brothers and Pops, and wish that I had got Maman's more delicate smaller slope. Pops had to leave school to look after his mother when his younger brother died of TB. I was never sure quite what TB was and it never felt right to ask. Maman and her sisters would bring soup to him and his mother and Maman would keep him company with stories of school and the lessons he missed. She went to school for both of them. When Pops lost his brother, Maman said his words died inside. He got quieter and stiller, so Maman made sure she had enough for them both.

The baby died inside Maman. It stayed in there still and silent and she knew right away but couldn't get to it to save it

Maman unravelled for a couple of weeks and her sisters from the other side of the island came over, taking turns to fill in for the cooking and chores and sit with her in the bedroom. It's amazing, watching women knit each other back to life. They were busy, but gentle soft busy. They worked like the weakness of gravity, a constant pull until Maman's feet finally touched back down on the ground.

It was dusk all the time before then, the lack of light would trick us. None of us ready for the night without Maman as our light, unsure of how another darkness would fall on her and for how long.

One day she just got up and started living again.

Not the baby.

Maman.

She just pulled herself right up to standing, got out a big pan and announced it was time to make jam.

Jam days were hope and spring, outside and in for Maman after the baby, even though it signalled autumn had arrived.

The gilded evenings shone through the emptying trees as the brittle leaves dropped for us to kick back into the air like a dry storm. The big pan days before, on the sink side as a reminder while Maman busied herself with the crops from the garden and tied up onions in the kitchen store to dry. The hooks of the store would fill and the empty jars on the floor would come out for a wash. We got our blackberry hook sticks out from where they sat the rest of the year, leaning in the corner of the store. They were as regular as a Christmas tree. Swiping them in the air with swooshes we headed out to the places we knew to be the best, pulling the juiciest fruits from the middle of the mesh of thorns. Purple juices, stained our mouths and hands as we carried the baskets back home, arguing over who had got the most. Maman would coo at us, at the fruit, and pile all our individual hoards together to stop the arguing, then we were shooed out of the kitchen to make way for the sugar and heat. This was the most dangerous times for our fingers and mouths, the sticky jam came into life with the caramel scents and toffee edge burnings enticing us to lick a spoon or put a finger in the pot.

Once David put the spoon to his mouth and before Maman could save him he touched his lips with the molten mixture. It stuck and then pulled half of his lip off. The skin dangling on the spoon like the peel of a plum. That was the lesson learnt for all of us, our temptation was always tempered with the image of the plum skin dangling lip of David.

His lip took a long time to recover, first raw like meat then scabbing over to look like a huge cold sore ormer shell, growing back underneath. If you look at him now it might not be really noticeable, but it still looks like he has smudged his smile a little, or a bit of water has drooped the line of his painted lip.

When the jars were full of the hot jam I would go and sit with one in a tea towel, feeling the heat creep into my hands, my stomach, my thighs, a creature sitting here, alive. But we had taken that live thing and captured it. We had taken a whole day and boiled it into sugar until it could last all year, even salty air on the skin of the blackberries. Catching them, taking them as ours, licking and stealing what fell in our baskets, our fingers blue for days.

Today wasn't jam day.

Today we hadn't captured anything.

Maman felt the empty net. Her empty basket.

I told Maman I would go up the far hill and spy to see them from there. Maman said no, she didn't want another of her babies going anywhere wild. I was to go get Pops from the Smugglers Inn. He'd had long enough there anyway, she said, and he was only meant to be checking whether the old sea tractor was still in need of an oil change. She said it to me like I was him and she was telling him off. Time had a different meaning for Pops at the inn.

Easy in, hard out. Like a lobster basket, except Pops was happy to be caught.

As I stepped out of the door it wasn't quite dusk, but the light was fading. It had felt darker inside the kitchen with Maman. There was at least another half hour before it darkened.

Instead of my usual trip to the well or the opposite way to the sea, I crossed a "t" or an "f" of that path and headed directly over towards the Smugglers Inn. The whitewash was glowing as if it had caught the light of the day in the walls. The windows were dark except for a warm glow at the edges from the lamps. Small red shades with tassels and folds that let out only a little of the bulb light inside. They had a warm fire feel to them, the lit hearts of sailors gone. This was the quicker route but I'd seldom come this way, as I would have to pass Mr. Willow's house.

Mr. Willow was our landlord.

Mr. Willow had a horse and trap, lived alone, and acted like life was sent to try him by moving too fast. He owned our cottage and his house and a lot of the common that wasn't freeman land.

We steered clear of him. He was neither friendly nor kind; he was the boogey man, to avoid. If we came face to face with him, our instincts would prickle. There was that time the brothers heard him coming so fast towards us, whipping the horse, trying to run us over with his trap. David had pushed me out of the way and Frank and John had dived the other way, dust between us and ahead the horse thumping at the ground and the wheels clattering out of view. I told Maman and Pops, though the brothers said I shouldn't. I was so scared he was going to run us all over again.

Pops laughed hard and said I had nothing to worry about, he was a grumpy harmless man. But I felt danger around him I couldn't explain. It was as if he had a smell without a smell. Something just put my back up and I wondered if it was only something that children could see.

Every time I went past his house, he'd be standing at the window holding what looked like a large hankie. He would wave it when he saw me. He would step from one foot to the other waving and smiling, framed in the window. I would put my arm and hand up as a hello but not move it, not wave back. Walking quicker, seeing him still waving, I kept my arm up so he knew I could still see him. I wondered if he chose times to stand by the window to wave? How long did he do it and what made him finish his shift?

Was he counting who he was waving to?

Sometimes he looked eager to connect to get a wave back, to feel like he was noticed. Other times he would stand there and be waving blankly not needing a reply. Waving like he was washing the window, though those windows had never been washed, inside or out.

I often thought about what it would feel like on the other side of the glass. To be the one waving back at me. I wanted to ignore him. But that felt rude and unkind, say someone you dislike shakes your hand, you don't want to give them your hand, but you do. Show them how you have been forced by your own manners to do it.

That's how I waved at Mr. Willow. I would put my hand up, more like a stop sign.

Anyway, Mr. Willow's was in front of me and I needed him gone out of my mind and out of my route to Pops. I looked to check he wasn't outside the house.

He wasn't.

Back to my task. Get past this dark house. Get over where there are people at the inn. Get to Pops, get it done and get back to Maman.

Tonight I needed to stop Maman's dusky thoughts.

I took a breath and held it so he wouldn't smell me or hear me and ran past the house. No sign of him at the window. Such a relief. I didn't want to look back. I always feel like someone's behind me. That's why I can run so fast.

I kept on, faster towards the white of the inn. It was shining like a lighthouse on the tip of the velvet-dark common. I wouldn't look back in case he was there silhouetted on the path. In case the horse and trap were coming for me in a chariot charge. My heart was beating, a bird flapping its wings hard to get up to the good air. Banging in my chest, feathers hitting at my throat.

Chapter 5

Pops was at the Smugglers Inn. Of course he was. It was the only pub on this cove and the owners knew it. There is nothing like no competition to rest thick dust on any improvements. Decor and objects were the same as they always had been and presumably always would be. Each wall, like an open page, would become a little more yellow, a little dirtier and dark. The little red material lamps in the small front windows were on in the day as well as the night and they seemed glowing with ideas in the white wash front face of the pub. The building leaned its way down the hill and the steps into it were like side on wedges of cheese. The middle of the step worn into a little shallow bowl, catching watery rock pools from the drips of the hanging baskets.

Yes, Pops was in there, and Maman wanted him out. She'd asked me to go get him. I looked into the window so I could make a route straight to him.

It was always so smoky in there, a permanent mist settling half way across from the ceiling and the floor. The carpet was sticky and red, it was hot with the fireplaces and the thick bodies sat drinking, and it felt like being digested inside a dragon or something.

I took a deep breath and walked straight in.

Pops was two from the end of the bar. His glass was half full. He hadn't seen me yet. He was looking at the paper on the bar and saying something to the woman by the till. She laughed, but it wasn't a joke that had tickled her. It was more like a cough once to clear a throat.

She looked at me.

Pops looked over.

"Maman wants you home, Pops."

"Why?" He replied.

"I don't know. She told me to get you."

I shifted.

"Well, go ask her what she wants," he said. He spoke differently to me here and I knew I couldn't say anything back to him. So I walked out of the mouth of the pub with its bad breath and began back down the hill towards the common.

How could I go back to Maman and ask her what she wanted? I was stuck between them and the places they were. So instead of choosing, I started to walk up the cliff path behind the pub.

The sandy path was worn, flat grass from feet. It sloped up and then snaked round the bend at the top and out of sight. The grasses looked so soft from the bottom of the hill, but up here your legs rubbed up to those razors, they spiked at you just like the brothers get at each other and me.

There's more wind at the very top. Already my dress was blowing, a clapping cloth sound.

If the island could lift itself up even higher than the ormering tide went out, lift right out of the sea, then the winds would whip even harder. I wondered if our island did lift out of the sea. Would it have a big root like a tooth being pulled?

Would there be blood?

The brothers said there was blood inside all of the concrete walls the soldiers put up. They said the walls were to distract from the tunnels. Walls were truths and tunnels were lies. I knew that china cups are made from bone, but I had never heard that concrete needed blood. Maybe that's why there is a war?

The brothers would often say things to me and watch the confusion on my face. John would rub the wrinkle of skin above my nose, making me aware of my frown. I got better at not screwing up my face. I got better at being in a tunnel and making them think I was on a wall.

They were ants down there, Maman, Pops, the brothers; and I was nearly at the top of the cliff.

Because there are no street lights this side of the island, our skies go dark. So dark it's like looking inside a hole or a well or a tunnel. Up over the hill and north towards the main town the street lights start as the houses get closer together. But here nothing has changed. Time has stood still and it's as empty as the whole island used to be all over.

Our lonely cove reflects up its darkness to let the stars carve their light all the way back down and sparkle like little silver fish on the sea.

On the beach at night, the sea moves like a dark animal, the waves' sloping sides lit by the moonlight as it runs towards us. The sea keeps its blue and green memories for the next day.

The edges of the rocks smudge into the darkness and the size of the island becomes less precise. Six miles by five. If you close your eyes and walk as straight as you can, you will always get to the sea. The sea has shaped the island, taking nibbles out of it, pebble by pebble until rock cliffs fell into the sea. We all know how big it is. We say the size of our island to people, like it explains what it is. I have never thought that my height or size of my head explains me.

"Islands are stranded and conquered."

I wrote that once in yellow pencil on a piece of paper. I took the time with the letters, putting it in speech marks so it had a voice and it made me feel so very grown up to write it. Then I went over it in black because yellow isn't a grown up colour.

Our beautiful island is part of a small group. The two main islands hate each other because they think they are better than the other. The islanders stay loyal to their islands and do the same by hating on the other people. There are other islands here, they get smaller and smaller til some are rocks that will never be lived on. Maman told us about hermits and saints who used to go and live on islands to find God. They would get food brought to them, and think this solitude would bring them closer to God or God closer to them.

Maman said she would rather be close to her family than be alone but closer to God.

"Who would listen to her thoughts?" she would ask. "Who would take her words and put them away into a drawer so she could sleep?"

We knew she was talking about Pops there. His quiet, like the cove, was a harbour, as soft as the semi-circled waves that lap on a calm day into the arc of the walls. He held Maman in those same arcing lines like the outside of a mussel shell. Hard and calcified ready to close around the softness of Maman at any sign of danger.

Not everyone sees Pops that way. Maman's sisters thought Maman could have done better, just like most people would choose the next bay over to visit instead of ours. You could pass through the other bay, to somewhere else, as the road went all the way along the front and out the other side.

Our bay was a big cup that held our life, sloshing around like tea.

It was the hardest bay to get into and out of, with the hills and the cliff cutting it off both by boat and road and so the people who settled here didn't leave.

I guess it was too much bother to get all they brought in back out again. We still had visitors and tourists who braved the steep twist down and in, but nothing like the amount on the other beaches. Once you got down, the only way out was to go the same way back. Like a trap.

Chapter 6

John, Frank and David were my brothers. Most of the time they were parcelled together.

"Hey, I saw your brothers!"

"Tell your mum that she needs to sort out your brothers."

"Where are the brothers?"

"What have the brothers done now?"

It was as if they were inseparable, and in many ways they were. They had shared Maman to come into this world and made her belly stretch so much that the elastic never quite came back. That's what she would say to me when I would paw at the softness. She said I had a bigger room in her to grow because of those three. John, Frank, David — always said that way round because that's how they arrived.

John not only calls himself the oldest but looks that way too. I think he was sucking really hard to get most of the good stuff first. That's how John is, grabs the biggest slice first. Then Frank came out next, so he was in the middle. I know that franc is the name of a French coin. Well, full face-on Frank looked fine, but when you turned him sideways, he was so thin, just like a coin. He had the sharpest elbows in the whole family, probably to make enough room in the middle.

David was nearer to my age by a whole two hours. He wasn't ready to leave Maman, or else he'd got pushed to the back of the queue. He had the nature of a wagging dog, happy to go along with things. Always ready to do what John said. If he had had any motto to pin to him like a school badge it would have been, "I'm happy if you're happy." He was soft and warm and pleasant and I would always go to him first if I had to tell "the brothers" something from Maman or Pops. Then it would be his job to convince the other two. John and Frank talked over David a lot, like his gentleness was a weakness.

But people rarely saw them as three separate people. They were a gang. And they were rarely apart, so all their separate ways mushed together. I guess if you live in a body and share a birthday there's always a need to combine. The brothers were all four years older than me, so I didn't much count at all. Minutes and seconds mattered to them, who got in first; it was always a competition.

Before the soldiers came, Maman said she could see right out to sea from the common, but when they came they fortified our island. Pops drinks fortified wine for the iron and I guess iron and walls are sent to strengthen. Just like Pops' heart had furred up and stopped the blood going round as much, the giant concrete sea wall had unsalted the bracken and the air that used to skim like a stone off the sea, would hit that wall and bounce right back. Halfway along there was a circular water hole for the stream to pass through and into the sea. This was our way onto the beach, we'd hunch our backs and bend our knees and round ourselves through it scraping the tops of our backs on the arched roof. Us and the stream.

Anyway, the brothers headed off, ahead of me, pouring salt down the holes and waiting for the clams to come up.

Soon the ormering tide will be here.

The sea goes out really far and really shallow. As if it wants to touch the horizon. It's my favourite thing. Walking on water, walking on a part of the island that is usually lost under deep sea, like Atlantis. We get to look back at where we live, from a new view, the blanket of the sea pulled back with all the pockets of creatures for us to walk among.

It belongs to all of us once a year.

We can all go out for ormers.

Maman says that when Pops goes fishing sometimes the last thing he is interested in is fish. It's the time on his own, the waiting itself. I don't even like the taste of ormers that much. Not as sweet as mussels or as fishy. Maman says they are the pig of the sea; Pops says they taste like veal or sweetbreads. I don't trust their meat, it doesn't belong in the sea; but I trust those days, the shallows and the sparkling sea. I go out walking with everyone for the ormers. But really I just go out to be there, in the part of the island that hides the rest of the year.

It's like the island has taken a big breath, filled its lungs and lifted out of the water. I know that's not true, by the way, it's the sea going out. But the sea going out is a fact that people are told and they just accept it. But where does that sea go? They don't tell me that, so if a whole drink of sea can disappear, an island breathing isn't that stupid, is it?

Last tide we all took our buckets, the whole bay of us, abandoning work and dressing in the shabbiest clothes like some filthy fancy dress parade. A shoal of fish, glinting on the wet mirror of the land, all walking out to where the ormers like it the best. Succulent seaweed and inaccessible craggy rocks. Pops and the boys lifted over five or six big barnacled boulders and underneath there were ormers of different sizes. On one there was two big ones and four small. A family, just like us. Pops held the iron rod, it was twisted into flat hooks at one end to wrench the ormers off the rocks and it was looped at the other like a shepherd's crook.

Maman carried the *pannier-a-cou*, a wicker basket made by the fishermen here and the traditional thing to carry ormers back to land in. We took buckets — the brothers, me, and Bunny. Not all the adults used the old ways like Pops and Maman, I saw garden hoes and shovels, butchers knives, anything to prise a gap under the shells. The brothers were wading knee deep further than anyone else turning huge rocks and shouting out if they found any. The urgency of the two hour window to fish got everyone into a frenzy to catch however many dozen they could. Even Mr. Willow our landlord was out — though he was dressed the same as any other day, it fitted right in with the dress code.

Maman had waded over towards Pops between me and the brothers and we stood there in a diagonal line out to the horizon. I had put my bucket down on a thick wad of leathery oar weed and was trying to lift a stone that I thought was small but its bottom was buried deeper down like an iceberg.

"You need help there?"

The words sounded odd and strangled and I looked to see Mr. Willow with a knife across his mouth held by his teeth while he held his basket and threw a couple of ormers in to it. He took the knife out of his teeth and threw it into the basket and I wondered why he hadn't just done that in the first place.

"Move over there, girl," he said, and shoved me over while he heaved at the rock. He knew my name. I was about to lean down and help but his strength was a shock and the boulder upturned easily. Only one ormer but what a prize it was. It was huge. Next to it on the underneath was another enemy, a starfish. Pops had found an octopus holding one in a fishing net once, its tentacle curled round it. Ormers were wanted by everything it seemed.

What happened next made me wince and screw up my face. Mr. Willow's knife slipped as he dug at the shell. It slid right across the palm of his hand and the wound dripped fast straight away, a line of blood tricking off the rocks in small splashes.

"Help!" I shouted straight away in shock.
Mr. Willow had put his hand up to his face and sucked at the wound. A line of blood like a smile smeared ear to ear across his cheeks and ran down his chin, the wetness making it look like more blood.

"Damn it, I'll have to go in now," he said angrily, and before anyone got to us with their wet heavy wading legs I watched him get his knife and slice two of the legs off the starfish in anger as he passed.

Maman crossed his path, lifted his arm up above his head and took him to shore to get cleaned up. The brothers were here, straight onto getting that big ormer off the rock that Mr. Willow had turned over.

John was getting the salt jar from the shelf. His arms branched easily up there. Even on my tiptoes I couldn't touch the bottom edge of the shelf. Being the smallest, I was always watching the action because I never could reach the shelf.

Maman had asked the boys to go down and get some razor clams for her. Even though it was a chore for her it appealed to all of them. John leading the way, Frank shouting which holes to John, betting which would be the biggest and juiciest, and David got to hold the bag.

I'd walk down to the beach with them, Maman said I was her eyes and ears.

John had used all the salt already before anyone got a chance, passing the empty jar for David to hold. He'd told Frank to keep an eye out on his holes and was heading over to the rocks to see what was sitting at the bottom.

I followed John.

Just by the rocks was a dogfish. It looked like a silver statue. So smooth, so still. Had it been thrown out by the fishermen or had it swam all the way to the beach and got stuck? It wasn't breathing, I was panting after catching up with John. I had to check a few times it was me doing the breathing, living. I held my breath to not confuse my breaths with its.

Yes, it was dead and still. I took a big gasp of air back in, felt happy and sad.

Its mouth, down turned at the edges, looked like it would speak French and its gills were closed shut. I bent down and stroked it. Less like the silk it looked like, a little like a cat tongue—or was that my sandy hand rubbing rough onto it?.

John touched it lightly with his toe boot.

It wobbled like jelly a bit then was still again. I stood up. I thought we were thinking the same quiet sadness, John and I. Saying a prayer for the lonely night porter of the sea.

"Bonne Nuit," I whispered.

John laughed, gave a huge yell and kicked it right in the belly.

The intake of cold air burnt the back of my throat like sick. His shoe was wedged right inside the fish and he was yelling and laughing. Hopping around with the silver thing on the end of his shoe.

My brothers, quick behind me, were laughing and slapping their legs, pointing at John who was windmilling his arms to keep a good balance, and also for the whole show he was putting on. John was shaking his shoe and eventually the fish went flying up back towards the rocks, its red guts coming out like shredded paper in a parcel.

The redness had been held inside that silver all this time. The silver skin of the concrete sea wall, shimmering and scaled, with us the bloody guts inside. Curving around the bay. The iron that holds within it.

As the soft fish hit the side of that rock, bile pulled up inside me and I wretched, bending over ready to be sick. I couldn't turn back to look so I walked past the three of them, back towards the cottage. All three brothers ranked and positioned by the sizes of them. John would never need fortifying. He'd taken all the iron Maman had and left the silver coin of Frank and it was always a warm bronze place for David.

Chapter 7

Why was Mrs. Bertram on the roof?

"The silly old bat."

That's what I heard people say of her as she bumbled and mumbled along towards the post office. They talked like she dithered with no purpose to her day, her life. She was as practical and forthright as Maman but she didn't use all the *pleases* and *thanks yous* thrown about by the other women from the top of the cliff who never seemed to mean it other than to underline something they were saying to each other about someone or other. Mrs. Bertram didn't have the right way or purpose that those ladies wanted and seemed to demand other women to have. I think that was her biggest crime. She didn't play their game. She wasn't a team player.

I liked her way. I liked how she busied herself, made her own way everywhere alone, there was someone else apart from me who didn't fit in.

There she was. Silhouetted against the darkening skies in her long thick brown dress, hair half-tied back and very much doing something.

I couldn't see a ladder, or moreover any reason she would be up there. From where I was standing it was someone on a cliff, on a roof nearly at the sky.

She was talking down into the chimney. She seemed elegant in her balancing act, her feet were on the curved tiles at the top, one curling sideways over the arc, the other straight and flat along the pitch. She was curling the wind off the sea, brushing her dress and hair back like she was flying. At the big dock, two years back, a tall ship came in with a wooden front and a giant lady carved to the front of it looking out and leading the way, blessing the waves. Well, now there was Mrs. Bertram looking the same, except she was not looking out to sea or land anymore, but down, straight down the chimney.

"Can you see it?"

She shouted down into the stack. I could still catch it, though there was no way I could hear the reply coming up the other way inside the brick.

Bunny came out of the cottage. He saw me looking up at his mum, I could see smoke coming out of the door behind him. It curved round him in the space of the door and then blew fast and upwards and disappeared.

"You okay?" I said.

"Something is stuck in the chimney," he said, pointing at his mum up there on the roof.

Mrs. Bertram lifted her head from the chimney and said, "Bunny I think one more hard poke and whatever it is in there can come out of the top here! I hope it's not a bird or a nest. Now that would be sad." She didn't sound sad. People can say things they feel needs to be said in a situation, without any connection to it.

Bunny shrugged his shoulders and put his hand up as a wave or a wait a minute or something. He often did some ambiguous moves instead of words to me now that he felt embarrassed of his voice. He ducked back into the cottage, leaving the door open.

Outside Mrs. Bertram stood back a bit from the chimney. I looked up closing my right eye to the brighter bit of the sky, my hand peaking a cap to see from the bright. Then, like a cork popping out of the chimney, out flew a piece of silver. It was like a soft moon pushing up out of the hole. It flew right up and I could see Mrs. Bertram arch her back to look at it just as the arch of the flying fish had pushed out of the chimney.

It was a fish. It looked the size of the dogfish I had seen on the beach. The one John had worn on his boot.

The slow realisation dawned on me. It was the same fish.

As if in a physical show of my sudden realisation, the fish came down on Mrs. Bertram's forehead. It knocked her head backwards. Her quick reflexes hugged at the chimney and her leg slid down a part of the roof.

I gasped.

She laughed, moving back to balancing on the top. Bunny had run out of the cottage door and was stepping backwards looking up at the roof. Smoke was now coming upwards freely, no longer smoking the fish in the chimney.

"A flying fish, Bunny!" Mrs. Bertram was shouting. "A flying fish! All this way up the cliff and up and into the house!"

Mrs. Bertram was like a child joyously cheering. Playing it in her mind as she said it.

"More likely fell from the sky, mum!" said Bunny
They were both laughing. You could feel the teamwork, the closeness, living together up there by the sky.

I knew the truth that there was no flying fish. I had that tongue-tied feeling again. This new secret stuck like a stinking fish.

"Have you seen David?" I asked Bunny. David was the brother who had most time for Bunny and vice versa. Bunny had helped David out at school a couple of times and that was new to him. Bunny didn't ignore David and his kindness

"Yes, I saw them about an hour ago near the tower," Bunny said, picking up the mashed-up fish and throwing it over the cliff. "I really bashed the poor thing didn't I?" he said to me, wiping the blood off his hands.

I pushed my lips together tightly into the best smile I could and nodded.

Mrs. Bertram was down off the roof and walking towards us. She was slapping her sooty hands together one on top of the other. She looked like she had cracked her head open, blood on her forehead, a tiny trickling fish gut at the side of her face.

She was quick down off the roof.

She must have had a ladder at the back.

Chapter 8

I was back in the middle, coming off the cliff, still not knowing if I should go to the cottage or the inn. Coming down the cliff, my feet and legs just took me at a speed that felt like my body was something different to my mind. It jolted mechanically and went really fast until I was back down in the bowl of the common. I bent over to rub my legs where the sharp grass had sliced at me. I licked my hand and rubbed up and down. The stinging was wet now.

Frank and David were running back from the beach. I couldn't call them the brothers because there were only two of them. I started down towards them, slipping on the loose stones. Night was coming and I wanted to be back at the cottage. Maman would want to know what Pops had said to me. I hadn't even gone back to her and I hadn't gone back to him. I was stuck in that choice of where to go.

So I ran back to the Smugglers Inn, steamed in and shouted to Pops, "Maman wants you now."
Without waiting for a reply I turned on my heels and ran.

Now all I had to do was get back to the cottage along the path.

Out just ahead I could make out the shape of someone. Oh, Hell, not in the dusk. Not the soldier. Sometimes he would be the shape of a tree or a post or a bush, but this really did look like it had legs and it was moving. My heart held itself tight.

Two steps out into the path and I could see it was Mr. Willow. He did well as the shadow of a gnarly old tree. As he stepped forward enough out of the dark, I took a breath. Completely stark naked.

"Mr. Willow! You need to get some clothes on you. You, you, you —you need clothes."

I said all this looking down.

"Rozel!" He sounded very friendly.
His rusted unused smile was sticking to his earthy teeth. I was now looking at his face and the sky and trying to ignore any of the other stuff.

I noticed the sky had darkened down and met the dark common.

I was in the dark with him.

"I am like this because I am going to go and have a bath in your bath."

"Does Maman know you are coming to our bath?"

"Well, she said yesterday — I, I mean a while ago — come have a bath, Mr. Willow, if you need to."

I remembered her saying that too.

It was last year when Mr. Willow's water went off.

He tipped an invisible hat and walked past me towards our cottage swinging his arms and his saggy little bottom at the top of his scrawny legs. He looked like a sad old stranded jellyfish. Wobbling along his feet not going exactly right on the path, jelly wobble.

The brothers would poke and throw sand on the beached ones in summer. They were cruel to anything that got stranded on the beach. They owned the beach and anything that landed on it was theirs.

I loved the shapes and colours suspended in the arc of jellyfish. The purple rings of the moon jellyfish. Circles making the four corners of a square. They were little worlds of their own. Suspending the making parts of themselves in a dome. I looked through the window, down into their whole structure, no longer floating but flat on the sand.

Mr. Willow was showing his whole structure and it was as sad and jelly-wobbling as anything from the tide.

He carried on to our gate and to the kitchen door. I heard a high pitched scream coming from the kitchen followed by a "Mr. Willow!" from Maman. I imagined her dropping some potatoes or a knife.

The door shut before I had a chance to hear what he had said in return to her. But I presume that she covered him up and ran a bath. Mr. Willow did things that were odd. I couldn't work out if Maman turned a blind eye because he was old, because he was our landlord or for some other reason.

I suppose a landlord is like a boss. They can say if you have a home or not.

At the cottage, I saw Mr. Willow looking out of the bathroom window. Thankfully the sill was high enough to only see his bare chest. His skin was hanging from his shoulders. He was thin, the skin was bigger than his body and it was like he was wearing himself a size too big. He was looking at me and waving. It was the same old routine that he did at his own house. But it was from ours.

Chapter 9

I ran around the back of the cottage and saw the door open, the light on and Maman shouting at Frank and David.

"Where is he? Where is John?" she said

"We don't know," said Frank. "We were all going in different directions, playing, hide and seek, playing jump on backs."

I looked at them both, their heads hanging low.

"You can't have just lost your brother," Maman cried out. She was waving her hand as if she was summoning him out of the air. I stood in the doorway.

"What's happening?" I said as a way of announcing myself to them all.

"Shut the door, Rozel," said Maman. "Have you seen John?"

"No, Maman, but Bunny said he saw them all about an hour ago."

"Bunny? Where was Bunny?"

"Up on his roof." I'd said it wrong, but there was no time to say that it had been Mrs. Bertram, or for that matter any of what had gone on.

Maman seemed so blown about. Her mind was batting backwards and forwards. We were standing in the room with her body but her head was somewhere different. You could feel her sway with all the information and none of it making sense. The whole thing didn't make sense.

Maman was wringing out the tea towel as she spoke. "Where the Hell is Pops?"

It was like the room had got stuck in a groove and just kept circling the same question. *Where was John?*

Maman's chest was lifting upwards in her dress. Her lungs were taking in more and more air in gulps. She'd take a deep pull inwards, away from the shore and then come in but not as far each time.

The tide was going out.

The boys were still. So still. They were never this still. Everyone was lost, including John.

Maman had to sit down. We stood around her. There was a need to be doing something, but no one knew what that was. Maman was the only one doing anything. She was breathing and pulling tight the tea towel in hers hands and being still while her mind was out, searching for her son.

"It's not been that long," I said, but we all felt it was too long.
We needed Pops. He lived in this kind of quiet. We needed him to get Maman back to shore and we needed someone to start doing something about the unknowing.

We heard a noise, stood to listen, was it the gate? Was it Pops? A squeaking sound, the noise was coming from upstairs.

Everybody had forgotten that Mr. Willow was in the bath.

When Pops came home Maman let out all that was going on, like swilling the flagstones. She couldn't stop talking. Pops sat her back down, rubbing her back. He listened to what everyone had to say, silently making a map of the comings and goings of John. Building a framework to start to do something practical.

Chapter 10

When the sky had darkened all the way to dawn and turned around to walk back into the day, everyone was a bit quieter. Last night Frank and David had been worried but jolly — calling John competitive, thinking they'd find him downstairs, laughing and winning the game, sat eating toast with his feet up on a chair. Smug and keeping quiet about where he had been.

Frank said that John would do anything to win a bet and had probably climbed a tree or covered himself in mud to avoid being found. David kept saying how hard John would be laughing when we found him.

They said the game was still on and John maybe had fallen asleep in his hideout.

That evening no one had really wanted to go upstairs to bed. Maman didn't, she chose to sleep in the armchair facing the door. She said small sleep feels better sitting up.

I would come down often to see her in that armchair not sure if she was resting after being up early or she had been there all night. The chair was a russet orange red. It sat by the fire and when the fire was lit you could find that colour of the chair material in the hotter flames, floating above the kingfisher blue heat. Licking around the black frame of the fireplace hungry for more wood.

Pops said nothing that night.

He went out several times in different directions from the cottage that evening, and though he seemed the one with most purpose, his general look of unknowing made everything worse.

We were sitting inside thinking where he could be. Pops was out there looking.

He'd looked all along the bay. John wasn't there. He's gone up the watchtower with his bird binoculars and scanned as much of the dark slowly and methodically with the long reach of a lighthouse beam tipping the waves into silver.

He had gone up the cliff path to Mrs. Bertram's house. He had walked around and up the lane out of the cove. He had gone back to the Smugglers and asked all in the bar and behind to have a look out on their way homes. He had crisscrossed the common head low and downwards like a fox. Each time the door opened he was greeted to all our faces turning towards him, just as he'd seen the lighthouse beam, the black of the door cutting him out.

He would look at Maman and she would know before he even shook his head.

Maman was grave. Even in that first hour, in that first moment she felt a change in the air. It wasn't right.

I suppose that is what scared me the most. She was what I measured everything against.

I knew if she knew there was truth to him being lost, then he was.

Maman was everything.

The morning loss smelled colder in the kitchen. All the ins and outs, the fire throughout the night struggled on but the cups were cold to handle.

The kettle seemed to take an age to boil.

The boys had changed their story from competitive John who would do anything to win to cocky John who could have fallen thinking he could make a jump or a climb. The stories were getting wilder.

The island was being reassembled into lists and zones, places most likely for something bad to happen. The cliff top and the cliff edge, the sea, the woods, a dead branch that could have given way, an animal, storm drains. Mines, were there mines?

There was much more that needed to be organised that couldn't have been done last night, Maman, sleep deprived, was whipping at Pops with all the things he must do, but repeating herself and running out of words at the end of sentences.

Three policemen from the main town had arrived by 9am.

Many other islanders, a lot from the Smugglers Inn had come to form a line to brush every corner for John.

Two of the fishing boats were set with their nets slung on deck, empty and dry.

Bunny and Mrs. Bertram had knocked, come in very briefly, seeing all the people in the kitchen and said they would scan all the clifftops. They were dressed like explorers, wool hats, binoculars, boots and I was tempted to go with them but I knew I had to stay with Maman.

She was the pin in the map that everyone would ribbon back to.

"And what if John made his way home and no one was there?" she said to no one in particular. "I need to be home for him."
She had the toughest job as there was little distracting her from the John-shaped space in the house.

When I have lost something I retrace my steps, remember where I was, what I was doing. Feel with the memories in my hands what I put down, what I touched. Where the distraction, a drop, a slip caused the loss.

Finding something for someone else is entirely different.

You can try and think like them, though that is a lie. Questions like "What would they do?" "Where would they go?" roll around like thrown dice giving a different number each time, throwing for the double six again and again. "What would they do?" over and over.

We were at a loss.

When the second night came and John didn't, fear crept in all of us.

The question "Where could he be?" had been uttered to each other so much that now the echo of it was in our heads not daring to be said aloud again.

We busied ourselves with less.

The cottage was a constant in out of people, many I'd never even met before but Maman and Pops seemed to know everyone by first name. The harvest of their finishing school year had been scattered across the island, with different jobs and families but they were forever in short trousers and plaits to each other. First names and nicknames still stood. Who they were as children had stuck to who they were now seeing us as their past, our parents in the faces of their children.

I was often told I was Maman's girl, a cove girl, even in town, people seeing mother from my eyes. Maman's family was easily recognisable on the island. There were so many of them, sisters, brothers, aunties, uncles. Mixing themselves into new families and taking their faces to give to their children. I think Maman never forgave Pops for giving all of her children his nose. I had her eyes, we could look at each other and just know.

Now Maman's eyes were looking inward, they weren't looking out anymore. She was the distance. They were searching through the darker parts of her head. She would stare out, hold a hot cup of tea til it was cold.

She was less and less in the room. A paper cut out portrait. She had been downstairs all this time, not stepping outside since John had gone. So it was strange what happened next.

She stood up walked to the stairs.

Maman went to bed.

As she walked up, she said, "John *has* to be found."
I walked the stairs behind her. Did that mean she knew he couldn't make his own way back? She was angry with the world and giving it an ultimatum.

If I was the world I would be scared. I walked past her getting into bed and into my room. My walls and floor, the same as everything else at the moment, holding its breath. Do empty rooms wait?

I sat at my table to draw John's face from memory. I rubbed the pencil, twisting it from my fingers and thumb and felt the clockwork jerk of its hexagon edges rolling. I drew until my pencil went dull and flat, sharpened and drew again, my face close to the paper. It was a strange face that came out on the page as I leaned back to see from further away. He looked flat and his eyes weren't anything like John's. Someone else had come and sat in the place of him for his portrait. I rubbed out the eyes, to get them right and saw that even if I tried to draw over them again, I had pressed so hard the shape of the stranger's eyes would leave a dented ghost behind anything else I drew over.

I couldn't leave him without eyes in the page though. It looked awful, like some kind of curse.

He needed eyes if he was to come home. Slowly and surely I

arched his top lid, gently passing over the wrong dented line and took the shadowing of his deep inset sockets by his nose and slowly, slowly, he was there. I looked at his face looking back, feeling relief. I had found him on the page at least.

I walked over to put the picture up into the chimney hiding hole. My secret shelf in the chimney was the place in the whole cottage only I knew existed. Walking back I could see a light reaching out a short way from Mr. Willow's door, across the path in front and crumbling itself into the bushes on the other side.

Mr. Willow had said he would leave his lights on in the front and back of the house as a beacon. His house, our cottage, the Smugglers Inn, and even Mrs. Bertram's house on the cliff were singing out with a light on for the dark. The square saucepan shape of the plough constellation in the sky, but on the common. Corners of a cup with the darkness held within its four points of brightness. Four moons with their spilling silver paths joining together the net of light.

Chapter 11

They found him! They're getting him out now. They're getting ropes and ladders to lift him out. He was up near the top common the whole time!"

One of the farmers was talking to Maman but looking at us all. He was rubbing his head with his big worker's hand. A slab of a hand. A mole's claw. Fat and hairy and heavily hatting his head.

No one could understand how he could have been there unfound this whole time, and secondly still be alive.

The news of John was enough to deal with and questions could wait.

We all scrambled round to get dressed.

Frank was hopping around to get a boot on instead of sitting on the stairs. It was taking him so much longer, though it looked more urgent. David was pacing around like he'd forgotten something. It looked like he was ready, but he didn't know it himself yet. Maman was hurriedly making some sandwiches with thick slabs of cheese, each cut and then flopping down like rubbery dominoes and then sawing at the loaf quickly and vigorously laying sawdust crumbs in a halo around the bread board. Using both sides of the butter knife, conducting the sandwiches together. Pops was sitting on the edge of the table. The eye in this storm of hurry. I'd gone upstairs and arrowed myself into the nearest dress, pulled on my boots. I had not even bothered with knickers and I felt the breezy freedom never felt before. I guessed Maman would understand with the rush and I was ready in a round minute.

The door shut fast behind us and we were off. Off out of the cove. Up and towards the main town. The streets getting fuller, the noise getting louder and our family closer to being a full set again.

At the hospital me and Frank and David all sat in a row while Maman and Pops went into the room. We were told later by them that what the doctors could piece together was that John had fallen down a big hole. A hole so deep, that he had damaged himself as he hit the bottom. He had landed on his head and been concussed and unconscious for a long time, he couldn't shout for help.

He needed fluids most and then food. That was the first and most important thing. He was dried out from being stranded.

He was lucky to be alive, they said, and couldn't know at this moment in time what the lasting effects of all this would be, but that for now Maman and Pops should concentrate on the positive that he was found and in good hands.

John couldn't hear all this. Well we didn't think so because firstly he had a big bandage round his head that made him look like a giant ear bud and secondly because they said he was in some sort of coma from the fall. I hadn't heard the word *coma* before. I imagined it must mean something like a comma and I felt a rush of relief it wasn't a full stop.

We made our way back home at last knowing where John was. Pops let us out at the top of the hill saying we needed a bit of air and a walk before bed, but I guessed he and Maman wanted a private talk about John without us there.

Whenever I walked down the steep hill into the cove, I never want to leave. It was a bowl for the sun. The high long hour walk to school every day wasps steeply and the ground is cool as the sun slides up the morning sky to warm everything up. That night the road had had its heat and the long shadows stretched like our long strides, our breath finally able to be free now we had our John back.

Getting out of bed today felt the same this morning.

Looking out to sea from the hill I could see the ferry circumnavigating the island, which is what it did each trip. You got to say goodbye to the whole place before heading up to the northern island. The simple reason for the long goodbye was that the ferry terminal was at the south side of the island and it needed to edge round to the north for all of its journeys.

I liked seeing the comings and goings of that white floating square. I could count on my fingers the amount of time it took for the ferry to appear from round the first cliff, pinking in the sun and leave on the second. Sometimes I would play a game in my head when I would guess a number, then start to see if I was right. But maybe I counted a little slower or a little faster to let myself win.

I do that — change things slightly, so it's still the truth but a truth that leans a little further onto my side.

Two weeks after we got John back from the hole, the hospital called to say John had woken up.

Off we set again, the hurry from excitement, and we travelled fast with joy that we would be back under one roof. He didn't look awake when we arrived. He was lying on the white bed, as pale, starched and thin as the sheets and still with the huge bandage on his head. His eyes were flickering under his lids and I thought we should be more careful to say good things so I started.

"It's nearly blackberry picking time again, and that means jam."

I couldn't think of what else to say that would tell him what the world was doing.

The brothers (Frank and David had become the brothers again, even without John), shoved me gently and I knew that they were telling me to say something else, something different, but I didn't have anything. I looked at them, nodding my head forward like the cat asks when it wants milk or food.

"You say something!" I whispered. They both leaned back, shrugged.

Maman was sat by the bed with his hand in her hands. She'd been sat in that position for most of the time after John was found in the hole. The new chair she slept in was blue leather-look plastic with shiny wooden arms and legs.

John was opening his eyes a bit, lifting them, slowly, gently looking around. To wake from such a sleep must have been like clawing a way out of a big hole. The waking was under his fingernails like soil.

"Where am I?" he said dry and roughly.

Everyone else in the room looked troubled.

"What is he saying?" said Maman.

I looked at her, looked around, everyone's faces blank to his question.

"He said, 'Where am I?'" I said.

Maman looked at me.

"You can understand him?"

"Can't you?"

No one could.

Only me.

It was strange but then for everything he said next, people would turn to me and I would repeat what I just heard. It wasn't difficult at all but it seemed everyone else could not get their ears around his way of talking, just me.

And it was like that for well over a year.

John's fall had knocked his speech into a new language. As far as the doctors knew he didn't have brain damage to make him not as smart, but the fall had made his speech go odd, like his mouth and thoughts weren't wired. It made it hard for him to walk without falling over. They said it was like when someone has a stroke. He must have got bleeding in that one bit of his brain and blood had pooled and cut off certain paths. They didn't know if it would last forever or if with time it would get better.

Another week of visits in the hospital with John now awake, I had to attend all of them so people could talk to him through me. Most of that time was spent just repeating what everyone wanted to know. I was just John's voice saying what he said.

It got quite boring but I was doing something to help Maman and even the doctors and nurses were grateful to know what John said. John seemed oblivious to all of this, neither grateful nor annoyed at me. Just accepting that I was his tool. After that week the doctors said he was physically strong enough and John was home. I was kept as John's voice at home. Everyone nodded at him when he would say something, like they understood him and then turned to me for the translation.

Why was it only me who could make out what he was asking?

I was fluent in falling down a hole language.

Chapter 12

My head is lower than all the yellow gorse around me. I lift my chin up and close my eyes. When the summer sun comes lower it can warm right into your bones. It's slowing everything and everyone down. Slower walks up the hill cliff, slower longer days spent on the beach.

Birds stay a little while longer on the grass.

The seeds of the gorse are popping. Hundreds of tiny corks bursting out of bottles. Fairies with pop guns.

Tiny flies at war shooting each other and I am in the cross fire.

I am in the yellow flowers. The crackling fires of them. The last throes of summer, now. I thought the cold was coming with the sooner nights but this autumn day that stays in summer is the best day. Better than a summer's day in summer because you know it is a precious one and may be the last truly hot bright day.

Bang.

A shotgun fires and I jolt sitting upwards. At the same moment a cloud of birds lift off the brown ploughed field. A whole layer of black, flaking crows lift up with beaks full of seed. I can't hear their wings. I only hear the crackle and pop of seed pods expanding.

I lie back down and look up.

The crows are circling waiting to land, up there for circles, then safe back on the field.

Their black bodies are small tears in the sky. Ripping holes to the black beyond.

They are living shadows, selfish ghosts.

Circling the living.

I wonder, what would it be like to live in a shadow? I thought of John in that hole where no light could get down so low. It would have been cold, wet, desperate. If you've ever walked on the shaded side of the road by the cliff, shivering and then crossed over to the sun — well, that's how cold shadows are.

We were sort of living at home with a shadow of John.

The darkness from the days in the dark hole hadn't left him yet.

He was cold-hearted. He was frustrated. And like a shadow he didn't have any time alone. There was always someone there at his feet ready with a drink or a checkup. We moved around him through the day. We'd take different sides of the bed. And he angled himself against us, turning his head the way the sun moves a shadow across the room by simply working its way across the sky.

Chapter 13

The steam from the kettle was gaining towards full boil and the shaft of light coming in from the window was showing the full beautiful bloom of each round mushroom from it. It would form a sphere and then roll round and under itself. Almost the same move as when Maman would form rolls out of dough and push her thumb underneath and then turn over the small smooth curve.

It seems that all things made come round and rounding into the world.

Does anything natural have a corner?

When things move on or out, they go in boxes, in parcels, in envelopes, in boats. Hard lines of goodbye.

That steam was hitting the ceiling outside the magical shaft of light and the whistle started to blow one long tone.

Fog, fog, fog, fog, the kettle said, the shrill voice child of the foghorn.

Maman lifted it off the heat and the sound was silenced. John was making his slow way down the stairs. Holding onto the banister lifting the floppy foot up and down onto the next stair first, then the stronger one solid next to it. Each step, each movement was slow and I held my breath each time he made it down another step.

We'd been told not to help by the doctor.

"With more movement will come more movement," he'd said like a riddle. But it was hard to just sit on our hands and watch him struggle.

The brothers squeezed, nudging past him on the stairs, rushing out of the front door, pulling at each other and trying to be first to get out of the door frame. Autumn leaves blew into the kitchen, rolling in their dried curls. Frank had run down the garden put one hand on the gate and hurdled both of his legs to the sides of it and with both feet on the other side, landed together like a perfect end to some acrobatic move. David pulled the gate open swivelling his hips up and right to not get caught by the gate and pulled it shut behind him. It banged and didn't catch, swung open and then swung back again almost to a close.

"My gate!" shouted Maman at them.

David ran back, closed the gate to a click, waved, smiled at her and turned to catch up Frank.

John spoke and I translated to Maman. "Where are they going in such a rush?"

It was Saturday and there was a market on at the next bay. Apparently, there was a brass band from the mainland playing, cakes and dancing. Harvest time was for letting loose after gathering in the crops. Lots of the children in school were going to head that way and stay around and about for the day.

I wasn't sure what I was going to do.

The walk over the hill the opposite side of the common was too much for John. I didn't feel I could say I was going to go without him.

John was warmer with me than he used to be; he needed me to be understood. I could see the frustration of dependence flash in his eyes, and I could see he wanted to kick me in the guts like the silver fish on the beach.

He kicked the table leg. And then sat down, looking out of the window as he sank towards the table bent over.

His hair had lost its sun kissed golden strands. It had darkened around his face, his forehead furrowed with the concentration of simple tasks. John seemed smaller. His face was lopsided the same as his walk. One side worked a lot better than the other but neither was winning. It looked hard work to live inside John.

The kitchen was made darker by the bright window showing open blue skies.

I had an idea.

It made me shudder but it was probably worth it.

I shouted, "See you in a bit," to Maman and John, and headed over towards the Smugglers Inn. The dirty windows of Mr. Willow's house: the paint peeling frames, the net curtains, a grey sweep like an unwashed mop had drawn them. I had never walked up to that front door before. I'd always hurried past as fast as I could.

As I was about to knock on the door, the door swung open, leaving me with a fist in the air .

Mr. Willow. In a vest with his shirt open, trousers hanging on his hips and holding a hammer in one hand and a plate in the other. The first thing I thought was of him smashing that plate with the hammer, just one of the many secret things he did in the house alone. His eyebrows raised as he took a long look at me.He waved me in, turning with his hand behind him to beckon me in. I shook my head. He nodded his head towards the back end of the house. He was holding a nail between his lips. That's why he hadn't spoken.

There was nothing for it.

I went in.

He had a wire spring on the kitchen table and he sat down to put the plate into it. There was also a jam jar of nails, presumably where the nail that was still in his mouth had come from. A cup of black... coffee? Tea? I couldn't be sure. There was no distinct smell either way, only a hanging sweet dampness in the air that was powdery in my nostrils.

The room was easy to take in with only a handful of things, the table, the things on it, a chair. The view out of the window was of part of the common I knew really well but postcard framed from here, it felt very far away.

I spoke quickly before I lost my nerve.

"Will you take me and John on your horse and trap up to the market at St. Martha's bay?"

In his vest I could see what I had thought of as frail twig arms were actually full of muscle. Yes, the skin was hanging down, but under that was a washboard of hard sinew wrapping around his bones.

Mr. Willow looked at me. His eyes narrowed. His face folded under his cheekbones, his eyebrows stood out like tufts of reeds with his grey shadowy eye underneath. He spat the nail down onto the table. Put both the hammer and the plate down. Stopped. Took a sip of whatever it was in his cup and nodded. Then he smiled right at me, leaning in as he did, the smell of beef Bovril on his breath.

Hideous. His dirty teeth, the greasy mossy stones near the underground stream were cleaner, where it bubbles up before the bridge. Up through soil. I looked at them and tried to turn my disgust into a smile in return.

"One hour," he said and stood up. "Be ready."

I turned on my heels out towards the front door taking a sneak look into the front room, a half opened door as I walked past. All I could glimpse was an easy chair with a teddy bear sat on it.

Why were there toys in a house where children don't live? Maybe it was from when he was a child? Even then, why have it sitting on a chair downstairs? The front door was still open as I left, taking the first step down from the house I heard a smash behind me.

It sounded like a plate hit with a hammer.

I got back to the cottage and caught my breath. Maman looked at me, beckoned me to her, hugged me and rubbed my hair. She took her hand away to turn the tap off that was filling a pan.

"John do you want to go to the market?"

"I sisack dawn nawn thas I kwangit ontothiresta," said John.

"But you can go!" I said. "I asked Mr. Willow to take you in his trap!"

"You went to Mr. Willow's house?" Maman asked turning around.

"Yes."

"Did you go inside?" she said, her worry hidden badly.

"Yes. He's coming in an hour," I said.

Maman and John were both looking at me. Both surprised. John could go to the market now and Maman knew I had done it for John. She had always defended Mr. Willow to her children but she also was careful to not leave me in the company of him.

Maman had animal instincts.

Chapter 14

I had got so tired of translating for John. He wanted to ask questions to *every* stall holder about *every* item on their stall. They were getting tired of answering too; everyone was tired of it but John. I was sick of being the rope over the water between John and everyone else. John's speech was getting better though, bit by bit. It still felt like every word was too big for his mouth and the texture was rubbery. Too hard to bite on and chew to swallow, most words a spring returning to its original height.

I left him to it, talking with a stall holder selling painted plates, coasters and tablecloths. The plates were sailing scenes with a painted line of blue around the edge of some, others looked like they had been painted with a sponge, supposedly the foam at the edge of the sea.

I could hear John asking how long it took to paint one plate.

The lady behind the stall was smiling, leaning forward tracing her finger across the plate. Her smile had tired slightly, slipped and underneath I could see the tired boredom of someone waiting for the hands of a clock to turn her free.

Passing all the straggling stalls, the flowers smelled so heady I nearly walked into the wall. The vegetable stall piled high with bright orange pumpkins and striped squashes. The oranges and browns, globes, piled on top of each other, at the top, the smaller paler squashes a pale moonish yellow and as soft and delicate as skin that never sees the light. Bunches of carrots, tied with their green long heads of hair resting back and over the table. Under the table, leaning forward, were sack cloths filled with sandy soil potatoes. I paid for an apple and shone it on my skirt. I took big plate bites out of it and then held the bitten pieces to eat like biscuits. The crunch and the crisp juice, cold against my teeth.

I sat up onto the sea wall and swung my legs over to take the big jump down onto the sand. Just as my legs scraped over the concrete from the embedded tiny pebbles, I heard a noise.

It was a shifting, hardly anything really, I looked down.

There on the sand against the concave curve of the sea wall was Lucy Wright. She was a year above me in our class. She was draping her arms around a boy's neck in a loop. She had tilted her head to the left and was moving in towards his face.

I felt myself slipping like I was falling off the wall. But I was falling inside. Bunny was looking at her and unaware of me. The girl and Bunny and the brothers were all the same age but the girl, Lucy acted older. Some girls can do that, be old outside and talk older like the women at the shop.

I could hear my breath pulling in quickly, my blood pulsing. I was there still and stuck. I couldn't move backwards or forwards for fear of being seen by Bunny. I felt like that beached fish kicked in the stomach and stuck on the shoe that had kicked me.

While I was wondering how and what to do, my body had ideas of its own. I suddenly felt a dizzying heat rise up in the back of my neck and without any warning I threw up, fast and strong, up and over in front of me. The arc of my sick like a slow motion brushstroke, a confident line, made its last mark on Lucy Wright's back. A small slapping sound, patting her back in congratulations. Her back arched with the sensation and she turned around and up.

Bunny moved his eyes up and left landing and staying at mine without the usual shy back down.

"What the hell! Rozel!" Lucy was shouting. "What have you thrown on my back?"

My hand was in front of my mouth and I was leaning backwards to lift my legs up back and down off the sea wall onto the nearer pavement.

The heat in my cheeks was unbearable, a beacon. I kept low, turning back from the stalls and John. I ran towards the big hill and cliff that separated this cove and ours. I would have to leave John at the stalls. The brothers were there and so was Mr. Willow. Someone would bring him back. I couldn't risk getting caught by Bunny or Lucy. I could hear her swearing and shouting in disgust like a seagull. I heard nothing from Bunny. My heart beating was so high by now it was in my ears, pounding out louder than the brass band who had started up.

I was fighting back tears that were streaking horizontally across my cheek from the wind as I got up the hill. The wind got them out of my eyes and pushed them across my cheeks and into a small pool inside the small bowl of my ear.

I was wincing as I re-lived what had just happened.

"Stupid, stupid sick," I said out loud.

The muscles in my body cringing and tightening with the shame of it.

"Oh Bunny! How could you put your lips on hers?" I thought. "And this is what my body does?"

I got to the top of the hill, turned and sat against the incline, my feet pointing down the bank.

Below were the pretty tops of the stalls and the snaking of bodies moving from one side to the other. There was the smooth yellow of the beach, the clean margin to all the activity written on the page of the bay. I couldn't see any sign of John. People were hard to make out down below, just thumb print sized colour smudges. I could see Mr. Willow sitting on his trap. Was he ready to go?

Looking down, at the people milling under the covers of the market, in and out of the stalls, bees into flowers.

Two boys were walking together, pushing each other into the road and laughing, Frank and David. Even though they were the size of commas on a page I could tell by how they were pushing and shoving enough to bump about like insects jumping. They knew how to lean into each other.

I suddenly burst into tears, streaming down my face, blowing off my jaw. I was crying so hard my face ached and my shoulders felt the sky. Was I crying for the brothers or for myself?

Look what time does to people. How the dark content of them can rot or change til they no longer see who they were, or how they got to where they are.

John had become someone I had to look after for Maman. His fear of depending had slowly chipped away the strong walls of his leadership and it had left him out of the brothers' tribe.

The brothers had blossomed in the wake of this new order and were free to both take charge of themselves and each other. They weren't intentionally leaving John out but physically there was so much John couldn't do, and without me tagging along as his interpreter, neither one would understand him. Maman was damn sure she wasn't going to lose John to the ground again, so much so she kept him on a short leash, needing him close.

John didn't show any outward interest in wanting to be with the brothers anyway.

That had changed. With the struggle of his speech and his legs to keep up, a rising damp of bitterness footed its way up behind the wall. My interpreter skills meant he wanted to have me around. I was needed rather than wanted. Maman's over generous protection of John since the hole had done nothing except make him untouchable, his spite going unchecked. He had travelled back into the behaviour of a younger child, dependent and moody.

"Why can't things be the way they were?" I said out loud.

The words left me and moved off on the wind, carried far away and it was gone, quicker than any answer could come.

I closed my eyes and saw Bunny kissing her.

Bunny was mine.

I felt the hope of it.

I wished the brothers were still a three.

The burden of leaving John at the fair started to nag at me. There was no way I could go back to the cottage without him. How could I look Maman in the eye and tell her I left him to find his own way home?

I kicked my heel back into the grass slope. I kicked again and again

"John, why did you fall in that stupid hole?"

I stood up and started back down the hill. I just needed to get John home and then I could work out what I was going to do.

I could see the horse and trap, with Mr. Willow on it turn the corner to go up the hill road back towards our bay. Was John on there? I couldn't tell. The trap had moved under the avenue of trees that tunnelled and dappled the way out of the bay.

"Maybe John is there," I thought.

Long strides.

"Maybe John was on there!" I repeated under my breath.

Fast strides.

When I got back to the cottage, he was sitting in the kitchen. Maman looked at me.

"John has been trying to tell me things, but you weren't here. You need to be here so that John can tell me things, Rozel."

I nodded. His boots still on, he sat there, looking at me with his lop sided face showing no clue. Had he tried to tell Maman that I had left him at the market, or was he telling her about the day?

I looked over at him. He smiled back. Was he going to get me into trouble? He seemed genuinely content to be sat at the table.

I wondered if he did start to say things about me, as his translator I could make it up.

"Thongs first opine market go ont zell," John said.

Maman looks at him and then me.

"I understood that, John," she said. "Are you saying thanks to Rozel for taking you to the market?"

He nodded. Maman's joy in being able to understand him at last had brought tears to her eyes. I put my finger to my ear and felt the damp drops still left in the bowl from sitting on the cliff crying. Change was happening and maybe old John was going to come back.

John never did say anymore about that day. He didn't ask me where I had gone or how he had got himself home without me. You could even say that he had left me there that day, which felt better than me leaving him.

John was getting easier to understand. His language was either getting better or everyone's ears were adjusting to his language from the hole.

The next few days I felt hot and weak after the market.

But I said nothing.

Chapter 15

I kept quiet about the heat growing inside my body and concentrated on the outside world. The beauty around me was so hard to keep inside, so I would have to write poems or draw pictures or even just colour a piece of paper. The colour of a bird's egg, the silver of a fish, the red of the flimsy poppies shivering at the edge of the field.

If I didn't write it down or draw it, it might fly out and not come back, leave or change, or not exist because no one saw it, no one saw it but me.

I didn't want anyone in the family to see the all things I trapped on paper, so I would put them up on the shelf in the chimney in my room. There was a small shelf up to the right and if I reached up kneeling on the floor with my right arm up backwards I could get each new item resting on the one before. They were folded up with dust and grit falling from the chimney, peppering the top that would then get sandwiched in between each new one.

Once they were in there I didn't need to get them out again and look. They were all in my mind stacked up just like in the chimney. If I couldn't stop myself drawing soon, they would stack all the way to the top and flip up and out of the top, lifting up and off like seagulls from a nest, flapping and flying all over the island.

Paper planes, paper seagulls, drawings of seagulls turning into seagulls.

The last picture I had drawn had been about ferns. They take so long to draw. All the little fingery spaces in each leaf. The curling, sleeping caterpillars, fuzzy and furling in on themselves, before they stretch and unroll for the sun, their feet in the shade. They can wave and dance in the wind.

I make shelves and shelves of things I've seen each day, like the fern leaves I drew today that were opening for rain to fall and drink from. Concentrating in my best joined up writing, a poem about the rain within a red frame. The pen seemed to be writing without my help. My ears were burning and itching and my head still felt hot.

It was so cooling to be writing about the rain.

The rain that won't stop.

Drop drop drop.

coming down and the trees,

past the garden are bent with it.

Wood pigeons on the cherry tree

are dark purple wet pieces of clouds

Broken off and snagged on the tree.

The sky is lifting up with no rain

Holding it down

Lightens its load on us.

I'm with rain.

I'm with pigeons.

Then I had drawn a fern leaf at the bottom and in my best joined up writing again, made the whole set of words make a square.

I laughed while doing it because nature never makes squares.

I stood up, dizzy, the paper seemed to be heavier since I wrote on it. Would this poem and drawing press down on the other drawings like a book on pressed flowers? When I leaned forward to get my arm back and up onto the inside shelf, my arm became too heavy, like it was filling with water or lead. My eyes sore and swelling, feeling too big for my sockets. My neck burnt and my head was dropped, unable to get back up onto its shoulders.

Holding onto the walls, I made it into the bathroom, splashing my face with water, flinching at the cold water onto the heat of my skin. Washing the soot off the back of my arm (from placing the poem in its hiding place), I noticed some red dots on my arm. They didn't look like insect bites or the bubbly lumps of nettle stings. They were red and the more I looked the more I saw, almost joining up to make red skin.

My throat was too sore to shout. And I walked down stairs to ask Maman what she thought it was.

"Dear grief," she exclaimed, pulling me to the lighter part of the room to look properly.

Off we went to the doctors.

Sat in the same waiting room when I'd broken my arm, I watched the different ways people's legs hugged chairs.

The man in front had put his either side and had turned his feet around and curling them into the inside. I thought he looked like a frog and I wondered what it could be that he needed to see the doctor with. People in the waiting room had secret reasons to be there. I looked around at everyone trying to guess, bodies can't always show illness. It has to be spoken, that's why we were here. Words are the first things that help a doctor guess. My skin was patterned all over now in those few hours.

Soon enough I was ushered in with Maman to the doctor's room.

At the wooden desk we had barely sat down before the doctor was ushering us out of the surgery. It was measles and I was to go home immediately and stay in my room. I wasn't to go to school and I wasn't to leave the house. It was very infectious and very dangerous.

We left through the back door and through the back yard. I was so hot and inside I wanted to open windows, to let the heat escape. I didn't even know there was a back door at the doctors. I had always come in one way, out the same way. We weren't to go past any of the other patients, the doctor had said.

Maman was walking so fast one of her legs looked like it was jumping. Her hips swaying, like huge waves on a stormy sea, bobbing up and down under her dress with the speed. She was way ahead of me holding my arm like a lead. She seemed to be rushing, to not meet anyone and kept that way up the big hill and down it. We were a cart let go from the top, freewheeling. My arm was aching from being pulled and my legs just didn't have the energy to move as fast as she wanted.

Once home she put me to bed in a newly washed, white nightie, that felt cotton cool and later brought me up some water. I woke up hours later though it was still light. I had slept most of the day and Pops was in my room kneeling down by the fireplace. He had built a fire and was striking a match to the paper and kindling.

"Hey love," he said. "You've slept all day. I'm getting the room warm before the sun goes down, we need to keep the window open all night for the fresh air, so if I get this lit, that should keep you right for the night."

I nodded. He had already said more words than I had heard in a long time. Not that he was a cold man by any means, but he didn't always feel that words did the things that he wanted them to do. He was actions. Fixing motors, changing oils, banging out dents in cars.

Bringing in the wood for the fire as the kindling started I realised it was the first fire I had lit in my room for a very long time. Upstairs was cold, it was the kitchen that heated the cottage. From the hearth, past the pans and the cooking, heat made its way through the other parts of the cottage like steam. Like steam it was thin and ghostly and it barely made it to my room in warmth, just the smell of boiling water or stew.

As I watched the flames, a kingfisher blue dart started to eat away at the triangular mound of wood that Pops had laid. It made a licking sound. The flames reaching round the edges of the wood like tongues. It was growing and lifting and the crackle and hiss felt like the noise of an animal. It was its own watching, changing and warming into orange and yellow flicks. Like a hungry animal, eating the wood, shrinking its pile down and growing from it.

I sat up. My pile of papers! All those drawings! All those poems inside the shelf!

The weight of my own head pulled back down onto the pillow. I didn't have the energy to get up and I couldn't save them now. I closed my eyes, all my paintings and poems lifting off with wings, up out of the chimney, flying and burning up into the darkening blue sky towards the sliding sun.

That night as the papers were burning , a dream froze me inside.

He was getting up. Shaking himself like an autumn tree and little shards of glass were falling off him and dropping to the floor. The high squeak of the water pail. He was smiling at me.

"You left me," he said. His voice sounded hollow and woody as if he hadn't spoken for a long time. It sounded like my voice in my head.

I stepped back onto a twig. It snapped. Crack. He started to groan and as he fell to the floor he disintegrated into tiny pieces blowing out towards the sea in swirls. His hand was the last thing to go. He was reaching for me and I felt its cold grasp go up my arm towards my heart.

"I left you!' I shouted at him.

I sat up and saw the white of the walls of my bedroom in front of me.

Breathing hard, it was morning, I rubbed at my wrist to warm the cold that was creeping up them. The gap in the open window was whistling and no one else was awake to hear the soft whistle. I brought my cold arm back under the covers, warming it on my belly.

As winter comes into autumn, Maman feels the loss of the baby.

Will I remember the soldier walking the common at night, turning winter on everything he steps on? There in my side sight, stepping backwards into bushes and behind trees? I had left him there and he should be gone now, but my nights, even in other dreams he would step in.

We had found out that he had tried to leave his rank. That he was sick of being hungry. Sick of building walls on top of nature. Everyone including him, sick of the sight of his dirty, tired uniform.

Maman had said that they wouldn't be here long. The soldiers would be sent away, back on a boat that wouldn't even skim round the island to say goodbye. They would set out a path straight home with their tails between their legs. Good riddance she said. She said they only had power because they had guns. They only took what they wanted because someone was telling them to take it. That she didn't see one pair of eyes in those uniforms that could know the paths or the flowers of the island or wanted to live here. They weren't living. They were all ghosts every single one of them in their smoke and brown uniforms. They were already dead inside and even a home fire couldn't stop the cold from their own memories.

Contempt is cold. And for all the warmth that Maman radiated to the family (she was everybody's sun), she could not find the human in the soldiers, they had no hearts, no rights. A woman with this much love could switch it all off for them.

To her they were concrete ghosts. Watching towers. Other.

Chapter 16

While I was ill, everyone else carried on with life.

I was left inside the cottage. The furniture and me, sitting and sighing. The house was noisier now that winter was bringing everyone inside. The crackle of the fire unsettled all the other things in the room that had no life with no way of moving out of the rooms they had been put in. While no one was around in the day, I had the chance to be other people, sit in their chairs, go in their rooms and imagine myself as them. Touch things they touched. My favourite place to do this was Maman's and Pops' room.

It was the corner of the cottage, facing away from the amber light hitting off the sea. A north-facing garden of a room, uncurling with ferns. The wallpaper was busy with roses, painterly flowering brush strokes of petals. Posies of three stalked with leaves, the collar of a green shirt around the base of their necks.

I would look for shape and patterns. They were not climbing the walls in the chaos of nature. There was uniformity to their placing. The redder posies taking one horizontal line then the paler more blousy rose taking the horizon line above that.

You could trace them going odd, even, odd, even in ascending vertical lines that would bend right around a corner of a wall and up til it reached the armpit cornice of the ceiling.

I remember following these roses across the walls with my fingers lying in bed next to Maman. She would put her hand on mine. I felt the heavyweight of it take a ride with mine. We would look at each other and smile. Without any words, take our fingers to all the roses.

I could never work out if the background was green or blue, it was turned down so much like a sound that had faded to nothing and we were there trying to tell if we could still hear it or if it was the ghost of what we had heard.

Depending on the light or my mood I would see green and imagine a wall of soft moss behind the flowers, softening the wall so I would stroke my hands to feel the texture of the paper kiss my fingertips.

Other days in the early morning cold light, the background fell to a sky blue. Then the background would be smooth glass or bone china, cool and arching back past the straight of the wall. I would rest my palm and feel the stone behind steal the warmth from my hand. My hand, a small version that could fit inside her same grasp completely.

Their metal bed frame creaked as you got in, engaging its muscles to hold you, a sharp short squeaky breath.

Maman's side was near the door. She could hear any coughs or the tosses and turns of us all and if she wasn't in her chair downstairs then she was here by the door ready in the night.

She got there first.

On top of their bed of roses was a red bedspread. A plump and silken square wad as big as Maman's heart. It had been sewn into a range of circled hills. I lay on the top so I could put my cheek to the silky smooth. Close my eyes and rest all my thoughts onto the feel of the material. The smooth nothingness of it.

Under the bed, a line of boxes down the centre, so as to not bother waking feet looking for slippers.

Before I had found the secret shelf in the chimney for my drawings, I'd kept them under my bed. Sleeping on top of these secret pages, magically seeping into my dreams. I had spent a day drawing birds in the garden. The robin on the spade handle, then a wren and its flitting and scattering, its tick tail making everything right with the world. I couldn't draw it down as it moved so fast and erratically, I watched. I put down my pencil and followed it with my eyes. It moved in clockwork, up into bushes and across the branches of the apple tree. I took notes in my head of its small head, the line along the back of its body to the upright tick of its tail finishing its little Christmas bauble of a body off. Once it had swooped away from sight, I picked up my pencil and began to remember it in line. It was perfect. As if I had drawn round the bird itself. The pencil's line, the balance and the weight. So thin and assured was the line I had drawn, as light as the bird itself.

That night I slept underneath the robin and the wren. All night I flew around in my sky dreams.

What was in the boxes under Maman's bed? Was their contents

the reason that sleep was such a shallow swim for her? I put my head over the edge of the bed upside down, my hair touching the floor. A square line of boxes under the bed. Names on top.

A box for each child. Baby clothes, knitted boots, a lock of hair in an envelope. Baby teeth, pieces of her children to keep, to not grow up and away.

Photographs of her in a family before our family.

Postcards with "greetings from" in rainbow arches across a sunny sky.

Pops' box had papers, a cooker receipt, a guarantee, a manual. In some ways the same sort of memories as Maman's photo albums. I guess they could reminisce on buying a cooker as much as sitting on a beach. He kept them for practical reasons, repairs, returns.

Maman's keepsakes were there to stop time. To hold us and sleep knowing we are there, within reach, her babies.

Chapter 17

"Rozel! Where are you? You're going to be late. You have no idea of time, do you?"

The voice of Maman travelled up the stairs two steps at a time and jolted me out of the position I had been in, half-dressed looking out of the window at a blackbird gathering twigs on the lawn. I had tried to find out where the bird was going. It lifted up in a swoop and went over the hedge like a fountain pen signing a name. Each time it would return I reminded myself to put long socks on. Looking down I still only had one sock on, books were on the floor and not in the bag and the time I thought I had, twig by twig was nested in some other tree out of reach. Quickly I began pulling on the other sock, skirt and slipping on brown leather strap shoes. Maman reached the door out of breath. This happens every day. Time gets lost in me. Even Maman's stern words couldn't stop my meanderings and daydreaming. Most days thrust on me, faster than I wanted to travel. I was always in the back carriage of the family train, following everyone else. Just keeping them in sight and turn as they did so I didn't lose them

I could see the three brothers, standing in the garden as a complete set, ready to leave the cottage. Racing down, I stopped myself but not enough to completely crash into Maman. She had turned onto the stair, her dress like a curtain escaping an open window as I thudded into her side.

"Sorry Maman. I lost track of time."

"What was it today, sweet pea?"

"I was trying to find where the blackbird was taking the twigs to."

"Well get into school and I will keep an eye out for you when I put the washing out, okay?"

Smile.

Smiles are boats and crescent moons. Sitting on seas of unsaid words to shine a bigger feeling onto the moving depths.

I hugged her, not quite reaching round Maman's waist, the comfort of how I still felt small in this softness, Maman's words to me as round as her waist, as round as her face.

"Wait," I cried to the brothers.

I was used to running to keep up with them while they never turned round. But they were slower now with John. Everything moves.

Am I one of them?

Maybe I am the cuckoo egg in the nest of all these other birds. Maman and Pops felt part of me, like my own blood, there was no way I wasn't theirs. I said all the things I wanted to inside my head like Pops and I pulled home round me tight like Maman. Maybe the brothers were the cuckoos?

All three were so unlike each other without a single thread of likeness. None of them had the same coloured eyes. Maybe we are just the four directions of the same weather vane.

The gate swung back on my shin sharp and quick and made me gasp. A fiery burn of pain. I rubbed hard at the bash and with no time to stay, I pushed the front of the worn wood gate. Worn wood by hands, the softest sea washed skin silk. Like kisses on fingertips, I stroked it free and walked out into the day, no longer needing to run.

In the corner of my eye, Bunny was coming down off the cliff. His dark small form was set against the skies brightness and the dark of the cliff made him of the same stuff. A piece of the cliff broken free and rolling.

Rolling towards me.

Chapter 18

It was two months since John had been found in the hole.

No one was counting but every now and then someone would exclaim how many weeks or months. Maman had looked at her diary, tutted and said "two months" to no one in particular.

Outside the cottage, the day was on its way up again. I was on my way to post a letter for Maman.

Mrs. Bertram was on the cliff.

She was cycling downwards towards the shops and going so slowly the skill just to stay upright was a sport in itself. Her coat blew out with the wind catching inside and it was like a giant sea was rippling up and down inside the balloon of blue cotton.

She slowed down against the incline like a seabird landing, adjusting the sails. An umbrella flapping open inside out against the wind. Balancing at such a slow pace, a tightrope walker, countering opposite movements to stay upright. There was sheer concentration on her face and probably on mine too, for I could not keep my eyes off her.

She swung her leg over before she stopped and jumping down, skidding her feet to stop herself, rested the bike against the side of the white washed wall.

Last week, Bunny had shown me the wooden box she had bought for him. A labyrinth. The two black wooden wheels at either side tipped the maze forward back and side to side to get the ball from one end to the other. The ball would fall into the hole before the corner every time he tried.

Mrs. Bertram was patting herself down.

"Box, box, box," humming to herself. Out of her pocket came a small box wrapped in brown paper and fastened hard, the knot straining at the top of the cross.

"It's my sister's birthday," she said as we walked in together. She had found some earrings in her jewellery box that her sister had always coveted. She told me she imagined her opening the box, seeing them and sliding them on with a smile.

"I really hope she doesn't think me cheap to give her something that was mine," she said.

I shook my head, thinking it was far more important to give something that you've lived with and would miss than something new that you've never had.

She bought a loaf of bread with the money handed back from postage, tucked it under her arm like a rugby ball and left.

I posted the letters for Maman. I had licked the stamp for the top corner and then licked the triangle of sweet gummy glue on the envelope to close. I could still feel the sugary glue moving around my mouth, licking at my teeth. A bit of me was going with those letters, some of the letter was stuck in me. Flying conversations wrapped up in paper, drawn birds. Outside the post office, the freshness in the air was drinkable, after the stuffy dusty gloom and I closed my eyes to the early sun, the red behind my eyelids moving small flicks of blood across in pulses.

Starting the day in fresh air was always the best way, I thought, breathing in hard. I sat on the wall by the post box and watched Mrs. Bertram. She got back on her bike and stood up on it pushing the pedals down to begin the climb back up the hill.

Beyond her, the last yellows of the common were brighter at the edges, the sun-touched parts. Green, brown and thicker towards the middle and the creeping-up green ivy, knotting and reaching branches and winning the competition.

The gorse looks back at me, leaning away from the sea, pushed by the wind coming off the sea. Yellow is the colour of memories. All Maman's memories under the bed are turning yellow at the corners. Soon the yellow would be gone, stripped by the wind, all its dreaming fallen yellow leaving, until just the bare thin arms of the bushes reach away from the busy sea.

Bunny never knew his dad.

He had gone and never returned.

He had left not because he'd been told to fight.

That's what Bunny had told the brothers.

Bunny built his dad's body from words. He found his father's heart in the stories from his mother's heart. John had talked about Bunny's dad over dinner one time. Pops had done lots of coughing that had interrupted John so many times that in the end John gave up. He'd said that Bunny wanted to know who is dad was and couldn't rely on the stories from his mum.

Maman got up and got Pops a glass of water and then started piling the plates up loudly which also made John cross. John could get cross at most things now quite easily but I did think it rude of Maman and Pops to be so loud while he talked.

I began daydreaming stories that Bunny would hear, Mrs. Bertram's voice reading in my head aloud.

"Imagine in your mind a strong big bear. A bear with smiling eyes. Can you see that?" the Mrs. Bertram me would say. "He would run with me, that bear, lift me down the hill and laugh as he did it. He would stride into the sea and the sea would calm itself. The talk of the sea would stroke his leg like a beach, and become as still as a pond. He loved birds and the birds loved him. He would see them and he would whisper to them about the best trees, the best eggs they would lay. How the winter wouldn't be sharp and cold, the fish would swim on the surface so they could just scoop and catch them with their beaks. And I would carry on saying to him," my Mrs. Bertram would say, "How it seemed that wherever we were together, the birds knew me as well. There would be birds in all the bushes talking amongst themselves. Talking about him, about us, about the weather, about all the things birds talk about," she as I would say, "But we could understand."

It was easy to make her voice talk in my head. I could make her voice say magical things.

Maman once said, "Children make up real stories and better stories than adults. They collect almost dreams thoughts, awake free thoughts that carry them into sleep, the thoughts that make sense when we are neither day or night, and use them instead of letting them fade."

I love it when she makes sense to me.

Bunny's dad could be a bear. He could be anything or anyone with Mrs Bertram's voice in my head.

It was spring. Optimistic lambs skipped and rabbits stood beside nodding daffodils that softened the edges until hope was jumping all over the island. Even the sea changed to a warmer blue green and the seagulls sat bobbing on waves like boats tied together. Maman said, "You are growing too quickly."

I'd been standing at the sink, my hand in the warm water swirling the suds around. Looking out for the blackbird again.

Two thumps on the back from the brothers took me out of my own world to hear what Maman said. I'd seen the birds circling and I was moving my hands in the water the same way. I was thinking about that morning. When I looked at Bunny I would freeze up, into a stillness, but it made my feet feel like they were dancing.

He was up ahead with the rest and I knew I could look at the back of him, all the way, without him noticing.

Near school he slowed down as if fixing his shoe. I walked past him, then he came up from behind and said hello.

Just, "hello."

Chapter 19

There is a French saying for twilight, *entre chien et loup*, that Maman says when we go out to play after supper. It means between dog and wolf. I hear it as one long word. It sounds like a knot to me. A long rope word pulled back on itself, through the loop.

The common is part of me and now it's warmer we can be back together. The day and night feelings inside me now are brighter and darker and I feel the highs and lows of life as a stronger taste.

Maman says it's because I am getting older and getting older means getting more feelings. I think because Maman and Pops can't hear me feel and I don't say what hurts, they think I am easy-going and have no worries. But that isn't true.

Entre chien et loup.

I am between dog and wolf. I am twilight. I feel like I want to scream most days and I don't know why.

The day I saw Bunny kissing that girl. The day I rained sick down onto the beach. That was me letting go. I feel trapped from the things I say to myself and never say out loud. My heart aches for what I don't know and don't feel. And that doesn't make sense even to me thinking it. I can feel my heart turning over like the car outside the post office. Its engine on but parked and idle.

I wish I had a sister to talk to.

The brothers. I do love them, but when have they ever said anything to me about feelings? When have I said anything to them? Never. We'll all get to hear each other talk about ourselves to Maman or Pops at the table, but we are overhearing, not being confided in. Sometimes words come out of me before I know I have said them. I am not sure if I am the boss of it all. The light of thought is tricking me and I reach out to what is solid and it is not completely there.

The common as the light fades is the same with its shadows.

We were playing hide and seek. I was behind a big hydrangea bush that had somehow found its way from a garden into the freedom of the common and gone wild. The light dimmed, as we carried on playing, my eyes not quite adjusting to it, merging shapes and patterns. The skin on my arms looked grey, blending in with the grey of the grass I was leaning on. Everything was merging into one.

The rock by my foot under the bush looked like a foot.

Between dog and wolf time. Between tame and wild time. Between dead and walking time.

Every rock. Every bough fallen from the wind, lying and leaning, my soldier.

The people who never came back from the war walk home in this time. This island is light and delicate like lace with the holes left in every family from the war. And yet I only ever see one dead body.

My frozen soldier.

Sometimes he gets up and shakes himself alive, walks stiff from the guilt of me not telling.

Death is a secret we never speak of at home.

Maman twilights into being a mother of growing children, instead of babies, and has seen more of death than all of us. Mostly in her dreams. The light reflecting in the window to the garden tricking her that children are playing outside. Not us. The other children we used to be.

She gets lost at the lack of need for her now, when there was so much need when we were babies.

Maman fades into twilight grey with her thoughts growing and nobody notices but me. The roots of family are what we stand on, in the dark they trip us up.

I look down, annoyed at seeing the dead soldier in everything, I kick at the root. Then I see it is a foot! My breath catches going back in me. I can only breathe inwards. I am inflating myself.

I step back.

I step back and see the leg under the bush.

The leg is in brown trousers.

Risen up from the ground, an upturned root?

I call out, "I need someone real here." I call again.

"What is it?" I feel a hand on my shoulder, warm. I know it is Bunny.

I point down.

"S-s-s-soldier," I say.

He looks down. Pulls the bush back. It's Mr. Willow, asleep.

"He's drunk again and he's not made it home."

Bunny was calm about the whole thing.

"We can't leave him out here, can we?" I said. "The shade of the hill will make him cold."

Bunny looked at me, his face questioning, rubbing with the palm of his hand at the side of his face near his eye. Was he rubbing the question away?

"I saw the frozen soldier. Before they found him."

I blurted out the words. I heard the secret come out of me. That old secret, out of me and in the grey twilight air, hanging between me and Bunny.

"What are you talking about?" Bunny said looking at me

"The day I broke my arm, I was walking here, and I tripped, and it was a leg just like today, but he was frozen, or frosted but I didn't know if that meant he was dead. And I just got the water and didn't tell anyone."

The words were hurting my throat which had closed so small the shape of the words were sticking like dry crackers, sharp and hard and they wouldn't swallow down.

"What are you talking about?" said Bunny. "*This* is Mr. Willow!"

"I know *this* is Mr. Willow!" I said. "But that morning it wasn't. It was a soldier with sugar frost on his eyes. I fell on him and there was no time to say it after, after I broke my arm, there was so much fuss, I didn't tell and he died, Bunny, he died!"

Bunny looked at me. He looked at me as I steadied myself. It had taken me out to sea. The weight of what I had said seemed to have no bearing on him. He smiled at me. He was taller than I was now. He smiled and I couldn't work out what made him do that. Why would you smile at a killer? He leaned down so close the heat of his lips, towards my heart like a light. He pulled away. Coming towards us. The brothers.

"Hey," said Bunny, in a gruffer voice, "Mr. Willow is asleep in this bush! How we going to get him out?"

David and Frank looked down at two legs.

"Can we pull him to our house?" said David.

"I guess we can," said Frank. "But we can't pull him by the legs or his head will get bashed."

"Okay, you two take an arm each and I'll hold his legs a bit and let see if we can..." Bunny started to pull him out of the bush.

There was no sound at first then yawning groans from Mr. Willow as he was heaved out, like a big sad sack from the bush he must have fallen straight through and bounced back on top of him.

I was just standing there, watching Bunny and the brothers trying to keep a hold of his slippy lifeless limbs.

"Don't just stand there. Go ahead and tell Maman what's happening, Rozel," said Frank. So I ran home.

Maman tutted at all I was telling her and she came outside to see the boys pulling him.

Mr. Willow was groaning, which felt good because in that grey light if he wasn't making a sound it would have felt looked like they were dragging along a dead animal.

The three boys got him sat onto the chair by the fire. Mr. Willow looked more like a scarecrow than ever, with the twigs in his hair and dirt stuck to his cheek and shirt. One of his trouser legs had ridden up to by his knee and I could see pale translucent skin. With big moles and marks, his skin slowly decaying like damp wallpaper. He smelled of sandy earth and whiskey. And the whiskey was sweeter than the soil smell. Like toffee.

He had foam at the side of his mouth.

"Is he just drunk?" I said looking at Maman.

"No," Maman had said. "He has had a seizure. He needs to rest in that chair, I need you to go and get Pops, he's at the Smugglers."

John limped down the stairs, stood looking at the scene.

"Hats he dong here?" he said.

It was me who responded, though his speech had become easy for people to understand. The link between me and John where I would talk for him had become a habit.

"We found him on the common," I said. "He's had a seizure."

"I con't beleef you brut im here, dorty o man!"

"John!" Maman said. "What is wrong with you?"

John looked at Maman as if to say *What do you think is wrong with me?* John felt wrong. He was trapped in a body with speech that was far slower than the brain working behind it. He was angry and bitter. He was the twilight child, slowly getting better, brighter, but never the same. His face reminded us of what fate can throw. He made us all nervous of the unknown. All the love Maman threw his way, all the time she spent with him, he was still lost down that hole.

"He stunks," John said disgusted. "He always stunks, is thur was no wate inn hus place. It's twice as ours and and, and it's just is him, conting his awn muney and spyeyeing on dus."

Hate was adding up inside him, it hurt me to see John with this cold streak. His meanness before his fall was given out to animals and plants. Kicking fish, tearing at bark, and teasing life from insects to cows. But since his physical strength could not match him as before, his temper fermented into vinegar.

"I dun't want hum in mine house!" he shouted to Maman. "Do you zunderstund? Gut hum out uvmy housed."

Each word barked straight at Maman.

"Your house?" Maman slapped back at him, then turning to me quickly. "Rozel, get Pops now please," Maman said standing her ground looking at John. I had never seen this before. Nothing had ever chipped at Maman's bravery. She had not one ounce of fear for waves, for winds, for hungry soldiers, for anyone.

I could hear the worry in her voice talking to me while standing facing John.

The brothers were sat looking at John, they were back into order with John as the leader. John was getting angrier. It was like his anger was feeding itself from the oxygen in the room, growing flames and he was succumbing to the feeling of power.

"I sud I dun't want dat *dog* eyn me un house!" John roared.

Everything was still.

"Entrechienetloup," I whispered into my closed mouth.

I stepped quietly to the outside door.

The room had stopped time and everyone was listening to the echoes.

As I started running towards the light of the Smugglers Inn, I imagined the scene back in the kitchen unfolding. I was scared that John was growing long teeth, that the hair on his neck was arching up and moving up over his face and down towards his chin. That Mr. Willow was the pale full moon, teasing him into a wild rage.

Maman our harbour bell, warning us of a storm.

I got to the Smugglers so quickly I could barely remember which path I had taken. The thoughts and imaginings had taken over the real world and made time speed up, and my legs as well.

Opening the door to the heat and smoke of the pub, I took a quick breath, diving under the water of it. I was swimming in and out of people looking for Pops but there was no need to search for long, there he was, as always, propping up the far side of the bar.

He looked over with a "what now!" sort of look.

I couldn't speak. I just beckoned him, waved my hand towards myself twice and stepped back out of the pub. What could I say to him in the pub?

That Mr. Willow was in our cottage?

John was angry?

Maman was scared?

None of these statements even made a dent into how the kitchen felt when I left. A beast was growing. I didn't wait for Pops to come back with me, I started running back straight away, to see what had happened in the time it had taken me to get to Pops. Counting each step, speaking a whispery jolt, a number each time my foot landed. The steady rhythm paced me to get there.

I got to the door. It was quiet inside.

I thought I would see what I had left, the same people in the same positions the same faces. Caught in time. John was sitting on a chair with his arms behind him and tied around his waist and onto his wrists was the long rope that usually hung up by the outside shed. Both brothers were sitting on chairs either side of him ready to catch or to stop him toppling. John's face was red like he had been crying hard. Or shouting.

Maman was over by the sink. She was looking out of the window, or she was looking into the dark window like a mirror.

Bunny was gone.

Maman turned round. The side of her face was red and swollen.

Mr. Willow was still breathing but slumped further down in the chair

"What's happened?" I said looking to the brothers

"He hit Maman," cried Frank looking right into John's eyes. "He hit her hard across the face with his book."

"It was the Bible!" John cried out in a laugh that sounded like an animal yapping, trapped. Then he breathed deep as if he could breathe the ropes loose.

David looked at me. "John has lost his mind. He wants to kill Mr Willow."

John was growling now. Snarling and baring his teeth.

"I wan that anmal out of mine house!" he yelled again. "Yous din ride back, Rozl, you din hear it."

John looked directly at me

"What are you taking about, John?" I said.

A gap between us both. Just then Pops walked through the door.

"What the Hell? What's going on? Jesus Christ! Maman! John! Frank? David? Roz...?" he'd started off booming, louder than I'd ever heard him speak and with each name had lost, got quieter until my name tailed off. "Well?"

All the answers flew out of the window with the question.

Maman walked towards John, she seemed to have regained the iron within her walls.

"Go to your room now," she said quietly, untying him. Inside it had the sharpness of glass, the coldness of wind off the sea and the sentiment of a gun cocked and ready.

John looked into her strong steel eyes.

He saw nothing move or flinch in her face. He saw the red cheek. The brothers untied the ropes. And John shuffled himself to standing and slowly turned without a word and went up the stairs. Pops didn't intervene. Once John was upstairs he went over to Maman and held her. She put her face into his shoulder as her body shook.

That night Maman insisted that the brothers sleep in my room with me. The fire was lit in the hearth again like when I was ill and I could hear no noise from John's room, only quiet talking downstairs between Maman and Pops. Their voices low and murmuring carried on until the heat of the fire and the comfort of the brothers in my room sunk me into sleep.

The next morning normal things happened.

The sun rose and woke me and the brothers out of their makeshift beds, leaving blankets strewn on the floor. Ashes left in the pan from the fire last night were cold and grey and silken. As I came downstairs, I expected to see the same scene as last night. John tied to the chair, Mr. Willow slumped on the chair. Maman still at the window looking at the dark garden reflection of her sore face.

But the chair was empty. Mr. Willow was gone.

I'd completely forgotten about Mr. Willow again last night. How can he keep being in our house but invisible? People forget about him all the time.

Pops was in the opposite chair, intensely looking at an empty chair.

The brothers were out.

"Where's Maman?" I said to Pops.

"She's at the doctors with John," said Pops.

"Is he okay?" I said.

"I don't know," said Pops. The sadness in his voice of those three words saying much more.

"Is it his fall?" I said.

"It would make it easier if the fall were the reason for last night." Pops said still talking to the chair. "I keep thinking about the Smugglers dog that got put down. The vet said, the problem is that if they taste blood when they bite, they can never go back. They will always be a danger." Pops put his hand to his mouth and I couldn't work out if he was stopping more words from coming out or wishing he could put them back in.

What if John tasted the pain from Maman?

What the hell was he talking about before Pops came into the room?

I sat down and cut myself a slice of bread at the table, spread the butter across and took it outside.

Chapter 20

Looking up at the cliff, I bit into the bread.

A different light was hitting the cliff. John's crazed outburst stood unreal in the new day.

Where had Bunny gone that night? What had happened in the time I was away? On the cliff I could make out a figure coming down the hill. It was probably Mrs. Bertram on her bike.

She was coming at a speed. It was *Bunny*, on her bike.

He was hurtling down the hill. At the bottom he swerved onto the top path above the beach and carried on. I watched him stop and jump off the bike and go into the watching tower (another thing left on our island by the soldiers).

He went inside. I knew that the steps inside took you to the roof of the building.

I went back inside the kitchen, grabbed my shoes and slipped them on. My heart was racing as I ran to the tower and saw his mother's bike flat, thrown down on the ground. I went inside the hollow of the entrance. The cold and dark always caved in on me in the tower. The narrow steps lifted up in a curve along the wall, the sand on the steps and the shuffle of my feet on each step took me up inside.

The shell sounds of oceans, whistling around and up. Twisting inside itself like an ear to the ground.

Near the top I could hear the wind over the entrance, whistling or more someone learning to whistle with their lips rounded but just the air and a faint note. I stepped up and out into the light, my eyes ached from the brightness and then I saw Bunny.

He was sitting with his head on his knees and his arms hugging round his legs. He hadn't heard me come up. I suppose the wind took away all the sounds of me. He looked really small and alone and I thought I shouldn't be there, I turned to leave and he saw me. His eyes looked up at me, unable to hide the sad hollowness quick enough.

"What's wrong?" I said over his head and past him.

"I don't-don't-don't — I don't know if I can piece it all together to tell you," Bunny said. He was sitting at the edge of the tower. I had been up here, lots of times by myself. Maman never knew where I was going then, and I wasn't going to tell her now. She told me to stay away from all the things the soldiers made. No one took care of them anymore and who knew if they were safe or not. Maman said, "They look empty enough to be full of death," in that dramatic way she had about danger.

She thought that any and every wall made in the war held a secret.

People went missing when the soldiers came. Their names never got said again.

But Bunny was here. He held himself tight like a curved shell. He was leaning against the wall, shielded from the crystal cold high wind. Most of the trees below were bare now, the tower wasn't alone in its nakedness. The sky was empty of small birds too, just a few gulls hovering over the sea. What was happening to everyone around me? No one was being who I thought they were. It was like a sea change. A storm had come and grabbed the rocks at the very bottom of the sea and landed them on the beach open and raw to the air and the sun.

Bunny looked up at me. He put his hand down on the floor and I took it for an invitation to sit next to him. So I sat.

"Rozel," he sighed.

"What?" I said

I was trying to be calm. Inside I was itchy. My skin felt hot. My back felt bony, sat upright. The concrete felt cold. His hand landed on mine.

"I left last night because I had to ask my mum something about my dad. I've been talking most of the night to her."

I noticed that around his eyes were really dark.

"I don't want to talk anymore, I'm really tired of talking now."

Bunny was sighing again.

I thought it, then I just did it, my hand resting on his leg. His hand went on top of mine and I thought of that game we used to play where one hand goes from the bottom to the top and so on til someone forgets that their hand is their own and loses. I thought of doing it now to start the game, to make him laugh, but I didn't. I held on and felt the warmth of Bunny once again all the way along a strand towards my heart without being disturbed by the brothers this time.

It was a good ache.

He turned, pushed me gently backwards so that I was flat against the concrete looking up at him and the sky. He was fully in the sun again. There were shadows, darker parts to him.

He said, "A hole had dug inside me, to try and know more about Dad."

Then he lay down next to me and talked about how he wanted to know who gave him the colour of his hair, who made his legs strong enough to run up the steep cliff path. He wanted to step into the footsteps that made him. To know the man he never knew. No amount of stories from his mum could change the loss he felt. I don't know how long I lay there not answering, but it felt like all day.

It was more like an hour.

The seagulls were still circling over towards the cliff and I came out of my dream and back into the day after yesterday. I sat up.

"What happened after I left for Pops?" I said.

Looking out to sea as if the memory was washing up towards him, Bunny began

"John was ranting, he was going nuts shouting that Mr. Willow had dug the hole, Mr. Willow had dug the hole... he'd dug it for him. Then he kicked the chair and pushed the table, he was hitting himself on the head. Then he was screaming 'get out get out!'. Shouting at Mr. Willow who still wasn't stirring. It was scary, Rozel. Your mum was telling him to calm down, getting in between him and where Mr. Willow was. He was saying that Mr. Willow was a dog, a filthy dog. And he was going to make him talk, make him pay." Bunny took a big breath then continued. "Your mum was saying John had lost his mind, why would he do that and not to talk that way about Mr. Willow. He was your landlord and that that was his cottage and he needed to give him respect. She kept telling John to calm down."

He put his hands up as he spoke, being Maman for me.

"John kept on hitting his head and saying you don't understand, you don't understand, you don't know, you don't know! That's when John just walked over to your mum and hit her in the face with the Bible."

He carried on.

"It knocked her backwards, stepping back up against the cupboards. She shook her head with the shock of it. The brothers grabbed John each side and threw him into the chair. 'Maman!' they cried. 'Are you okay?' Your mum said nothing, walked to the sink, took a sip of water from the tap and stood with her back to us all."

Bunny was lifting his chin up, swallowing, so he wouldn't cry.

The night I had left the kitchen to get Pops, I didn't see John tied up with a monster inside him or Maman broken inside from the Lord's book hit at her head. I didn't see the brothers taken aback from what they had seen. Maman told me a person can lose a grip of their sanity when they see someone they love lose their own.

The pain of John burning with anger was real enough to me even now up here a day later. Bunny had set the scene of that night and beneath it all was the rotten rug of Mr. Willow. When John was ranting and raving and making no sense to everyone else, in the little slumped curve at the top of his neck, he must have been grabbing at something. A memory slipped down the back of the chair, past the cushions, settled there, gathering dust. Bunny said that inside the fog of John's outburst that night, something came walking towards him. It made him get up that night and leave without saying anything. Not that anyone would have noticed, first from the chaos of words then the heavy concrete wall, cutting off each other with nothing but silence.

So he had walked out behind me, while I was running in the dark for Pops once again. I was somewhere ahead of him weaving towards the window lights of the Smugglers Inn. All the stories his mother had read to him, the fairy tales of his father the bear, none of it made sense to him anymore.

He kept looking ahead at the sea, the words tumbling out into the air. I was there listening but I don't know if that was the reason he was speaking. He talked to me and told the wind that then blew it up the hill towards his house. Their house, up there, looking pushed out of the way, all the way to the edge like where we sat now. The perfect place to see when a storm was running off the sea before anyone else.

Bunny turned as the words continued, now looking up at the cliff. He could see her through the walls, sat at the table. She was rubbing oil onto a pan with a cloth. It looked like she had been going in circles for a while. He was there too. He was just reading it all to me.

"Hello." She looked up with a warm smile. "What's wrong?"

She saw the confusion and hurt going on inside his mind.

"When I was little, I remember a face looking down at me. It was a man's face. And I just can't quite remember who it was."

Bunny hadn't even closed the door. Mrs. Bertram looked pale.

"What are you talking about?"

"When John was tied up after he had hit his mum with the Bible, he was going on about Mr. Willow's face looking down on him in the hole."

"Wait. Slow down, you are not making any sense, Bunny."

Bunny burst out laughing. He was laughing in the story he was telling and now in the retelling of last night. Sitting down in the tower with me, he was hearing himself and the crazy things that were coming out of his mouth.

So he sat down with Mrs. Bertram, back in the story and he replayed what had gone on. He said it was like she was at a theatre, listening to him still and silent, occasionally squirming and grimacing at the events that unfolded in our cottage.

At the end of it, Mrs. Bertram gave a huge sigh, sat back into her chair and looked up at the ceiling.

Then she sat herself back up revived from the pause and said to Bunny, "So what the Hell were you talking about when you came in?"

Bunny looked at me as if looking over at her and said, "I remembered a face when I was little, a man's face, was it my dad's face? Looking over and down at me. I've grown away from the stories you told me. And I don't think this man was a bear or a soldier or any of the things you said. When John was ranting I had an awful fear, mum."

He looked back out to sea.

"I had a fear that Mr. Willow was my dad."

Bunny's head hung low.

"What did she say?" I asked trying to catch his eye.

He shrugged, looked up at the sky said nothing. I leaned in and kissed him gently on the cheek; there was no reaction from him, it was almost like it hadn't happened. I got up and left. He didn't follow me and I didn't turn around to check.

Each step down that darkening staircase was so loud and the previous not quite finished sounding as the next one came. That staircase was a wintery cold inside at anytime of the year and I wanted to leave it with all that I heard on the top.

People were changing from what they'd always been, John, Maman, the brothers, Bunny, even me. The only thing that didn't seem to change was that Pops could still always be found at the end of the bar at the Smugglers.

Chapter 21

If John had spoken in his wolf hours. If he had managed to tell me then, what I now know, this is what he would have said.

And here he is in my head, his voice talking like I got Mrs. Bertram to talk, in one long go.

"Rozel, it hit me in the cart home, that day I had to decide whether to wait and find you or get on the cart with him. I decided it was better for me to get home on wheels than be dragged walking slowly by you up over the hill. I was sick of being tied to you anyway. As Mr. Willow leaned over and gave me his hand to get on the cart, I got a flash of a picture in the back of my head. I had seen him leaning down before. I had seen him draw his hand down towards me. I sat up there, with him, the sound of the market, the falling away of noise and the dimming of the sky ahead.

"How long was I down the hole? Days? Someone knew I was in that hole from the moment I fell. I think that person knew I was there the whole time. I only know that in that hole there was one face that kept looking down at me.

"When he handed me a cheese sandwich on the trap. I put it to my lips and there, there I felt it. I had eaten in that hole. I had eaten a sandwich. Thrown down to me. I had felt him pour something on me.

"I think he had pissed on me down in that hole. I can't remember it all. I can only shape him there. And as he drove me further up the hill, he was chuckling to himself. He was saying things to himself. In a sing song tune. He was saying, 'It's just you and me again, just you and me,' then nothing, he just drove me right to the cottage and dropped me off. And that was it.

"He came to visit me. In between the sleep I was in, the state of my head. He was there in that time of dream and awake. He was there, Goddammit."

But John never said that.

He didn't say a word of it.

He swallowed it down. And that time of silence drowned him. Lead weights for the hook to go down to the bottom.

His heavy leg scraped at the floor as he walked. Heavy eyes drank in the nights like the way Pops could slow measure a pint going for an hour. How long til John would be moored to the same corner of the bar, drinking down the things he never said, just like Pops.

His heavy teeth weighed down his jaw and closed down conversations. His heavy brain filling with thoughts, pooling blood into tension headaches.

Chapter 22

Maman walked into the kitchen.

When herons land, behind the rushes at the back of the common, they look like umbrellas closing. Well that was Maman today, in her winter coat, coming back from the doctors. Just behind her, slower, slower and more like a dog on wheels, dragged along by Maman's hand, was John.

I put the kettle on the stove and looked at Maman.

"Hi Maman , hi John, what did the doctor say?" I asked lightly.

"They've given John some pills. Haven't they, John?" said Maman looking over at her son.

There was a quiet between them. I wondered if anything had been said about the events of last night. John was not quite there.

"The pills will calm him down and then we can go back in a week or so." There was a long pause that nobody filled. "They're not sure if it's to do with the brain damage or a bleed that brought it on."

John started to chuckle quietly. His shoulders lifting up and down. It was unnerving and like a silent, shaking cry. I had seen Maman shake like that when her sister, Sylvie went into the hospital and didn't come out, but she wasn't laughing.

I look at Maman holding John's hand still just as she held our family together. Then I remembered the photo Maman had holding hands with Sylvie, as children together. She was the little one once. She was kept safe in the nest just like me. Two of them standing side by side, in front of the black and white common. Maman would say, when I asked her what it was like to have a sister, that they would talk quickly, with no need to fill in details with words to each other because they always knew what the other was thinking. They'd laugh and circle each other like seagulls over the sky. A chatter of hedgerow birds chitting, bobbing and weaving from one story to the next in a seamless flight. Sylvie and Maman belonged to each other as much as they belonged to the bay.

But Sylvie is not ours. I mean, she is our aunty and soft and kind; but she is outside our circle. Maman borrows her, knowing she has to go back to her own family, the one she has made. Them talking and laughing, I think of what it would be like to see Maman or Pops as visitors. I see sadness in Maman's face when she says bye to Sylvie and the same sadness in Sylvie's eyes, because they have the same eyes and I see them when I look in the mirror too.

Maman was talking to John the way people talk to old or deaf people. Loud but not a shout, clear and cold instructions. John looked like what he needed more than any pills or instructions, was the softness back in Maman's voice. But Maman couldn't bring herself to get closer to him, just holding his hand to get him from the doctors to here.

John was further away from all of us with nothing to tether him and I wanted to wind the rope around the peg at the dock, to stop him drifting away. Without Maman holding on, he would carry on getting further away.

John looked at me, his eyes clouded. They were dull and sponged with drugs to soften the harshness of reality. He was in there somewhere.

"I'm tired," he said.

He stood up and slowly shuffled his way to the stairs with his head bent forward.

"Yes, you get a rest," said Maman softer after him. "I'll call you when it's time for lunch, or supper, depending on how long you sleep."

There was warmth in her voice that cracked and broke into a high note as she finished talking to him.

"Rozel can you get me some greens from the garden?" she said, her voice still higher than usual.

I went out knowing she needed that moment on her own, more than winter cabbage. That night came quick and the next few evenings had less talking and everyone went early to bed. I was always the first to go up. Without talking in the house, the house spoke out a little more. Creaks on the stairs, scratches of things behind walls and whistling, an undulating tune where the wind sang through the ill-fitting window frames.

Water was filling up the cistern behind the wall in the bathroom. It was dripping like a tiny piano.

I opened the curtains in the living room, which was always the job of whoever got up first. The biggest window in the cottage was set into nine square panes, the bottom three were misted wet. I think, "That is my breath, and everyone's in the house." I draw a line through it. Tiny tears of water from the top edges were making long thin legs through the mist, showing a darker view of the garden behind the glass.

When it's early, the cottage is mine. Maman had gone to see Sylvie her sister. Every so often they have to meet. They talk and fill each other up, a reservoir for all the times they are not together.

Sylvie was Maman's pair before Pops. Sylvie and Pops understand that even if they don't exactly get on with each other, they both know the other loves Maman as much as they do. Their acceptance of each other comes from that and only that. Sylvie wants Maman to herself when she visits even though I know she likes to see us too. They take turns to see each other at each other's homes, to be with and without.

When Sylvie got sent away, people said it was for her own good. I hear that sentence a lot: "It's for your own good."

I can never grasp what it means when someone tells you that. Like they can see into the future.

When Maman visited Sylvie, I was little and she'd take me with her. When we would get home, I'd sit at the top of the stairs, and hear her tell Pops all about how Sylvie was lost in a fog.

"Who was out there looking for her, searching through the fog?" She would say.

One day I asked Maman this question and she gave me a smile that swallowed sadness down behind it.

She said, "In a way, the doctors were looking for her, but Sylvie also needed to find herself."

Maman talked in riddles that whole time. Maybe she was pulled into the same fog by visiting Sylvie. Finding yourself made no sense at all, how could Sylvie do that?.

There were plenty of times when Sylvie brought Maman back home just by talking her down. Their seas had undercurrents that pulled them back together, despite making lives of their own.

I think Sylvie needs Maman more than Maman needs Sylvie. But maybe that is because Maman has a never-ending amount of love for everyone. I feel it all the time. She leaves it in the kitchen and on the table at mealtime. She is our huge ceramic mixing bowl that lives under the sink, waiting for the Christmas cake to be made. Her creamy curves that have enough space to stir all the ingredients into one unit.

Each square pane of this window is a little painting of its own, a story with little live interruptions of life outside. The top right square is a skeleton fan of a rowan tree, still with some leaves but all the bright globes of red stripped off by a blackbird. He had balanced, bobbing near each one and grabbed and gulped every one down in one go. If I was as small as that bird, would those berries be the size of boiled eggs to me? I imagined myself on a swaying rope, eating boiled eggs in one gulp.

The top middle and the top left squares today were blue. Light touches of white thin clouds that are soon gone and forever. Three black crows with their up down clockwork wings, flying across the blue, their charcoal black leaving no trace of ever having been there.

The bottom three panes, all shared a tiny bit of the blue sky at the very top, then below it went across in ruler width lines. Banks of trees, then hedges and bushes, all sizes and heights, and all the greens there are by type of leaf or morning sun hitting it. The year is cooling down. The creeping frost on the window will burn off inside and outside on the meadow and trees by the time everyone else in our cottage wakes up, but it will settle in over the next few weeks and last until after breakfast. Maman and her sisters will sit with their morning coffee, talking billows of smoky warm words into the cold air.

Chapter 23

As John's senses were being dulled by pills and hurting from Maman's cold voice, mine were blossoming.

At least, it felt like blossom, pinky clean against a blue china bowl sky. Delicate clumps of feelings blown away at any moment like confetti. I felt open and light. The winter months had been dark with us all hibernating in the cottage. The steaming broths and warm fires, had kept the family close and Maman had needed it. The world had got smaller and safer at last. As the new year opened, we uncurled like leaves,

Bunny and I met more times on the tower. Maman was used to me going off by myself, so it wasn't difficult to get to meet in secret. I'd anxiously look around for anyone looking before entering the dark staircase of the tower, it felt so deliciously secret, though there was no reason to make it that.

Maman says, "A secret you share has none of the weight of one that you carry alone." She'd then say, "You can give it away with a flash of the eyes, or a knowing laugh. Or by knowing someone so well that it just comes to you like a letter delivered right to your mind."

I loved it when Maman would be cooking and talking herself round in circles. It didn't always make sense to anyone but she was thinking aloud and the melody was enough.

There was really no need for me and Bunny to meet in secret. None would have disapproved, I don't think; but there was a sweet grown up taste from no one knowing that we met.

It was good to meet at the tower. No one lived near there. The people who had built it had gone, so it was ours to take. The reason it was built there was for the soldiers to watch the beach and the bay and out to sea. Now it watched no one.

Everyone still calls it the watching tower. You can see so much of the coming and going of the coves without anyone noticing you spying.

How often do I look up in a day? At the birds flying, catching my eye, at the cliff with Mrs. Bertram on her bike. I liked it there, looking down at things that were usually above me. Looking down on people made normal things seem less real. People were clockwork walking on hand drawn roads, toy cars moving from the push of a hand. Even the sea with its shadows and depths felt like a puddle to splash in. The cliff is higher than the tower. At most, up here, we were up to its chest. I put my hand flat on the top of my head and slid it forward to check my height on top of the tower to the cliff's height, like you do in the family, especially when you are the youngest, to show you can grow too. I'd stand on my tip toes, edging myself forward to get to where they were, but the brothers grew in parallel to me, and I'll never catch them up.

The thing about being the youngest is growing isn't the same as when you're the eldest. They're already ahead. I never saw anyone in the family as a baby or move into different stages of their life. I guess that is why the baby of a family will remain in the minds of everyone as a baby.

I know there have been times when I have played it to my advantage.

Sometimes the brothers would complain to Maman if they thought I wasn't doing as much as they were and Maman would say that it was because I was younger. She would never say it was because I was a girl. Maman never thought that way.

A lot of the other girls at school did think that way. The ones with the plain English surnames. They would talk to each about the way girls should behave, the way their mothers told them to behave. They would wear clothes that couldn't get messed up. They would look at my scruffy skirt and boots and think I should be pitied.

Maman didn't go for those stiff prisons for me. She knew that if I wanted to climb a tree or walk up the cliff there wasn't going to be a dress or a skirt that would stop me. She could darn up my socks, and sew up my skirt. I don't know what I would do if the clothes I wore told me what I could and couldn't do. It seemed like an awful place to be.

My laced up boots had a deep heel that was perfect for getting a first hook onto a branch to then get a swing in and up the rest of the way up. I would tuck my skirt up into the edge of my knickers so I could stretch to the highest branch and see where I was going. Sometimes it would come loose and the skirt would flop right over my head and I would be in a cotton tent of darkness unable to see where I could get to next. And I would have to turn myself over the right way for the skirt to drop again.

Maman didn't play by the rules of what girls should be.

I would help with the cooking and cleaning, but that came naturally, not forced. It was a time when I could be side by side to Maman. I would watch and learn and do as she did. The way she would hold a carrot in her hand from wrist to tip and then having the knife flat take off the whisper of the skin. So translucent, so thin. Wasting as little as possible. How she could just run the new potatoes under the tap and scrape the skin into reams with her thumb nail.

All these things I learned to do by watching her.

Maman's ability to keep a house and work was nothing to do with being a woman. Her arms were like ham joints, getting so thick at the top by her shoulders that often she would take a nick out of the sleeves of her dresses so they wouldn't cut in to her skin. Vegetables came from our soil to the table. The digging up, the scrubbing, the peeling, the cooking in big pans full of water, then onto plates. Maman was the house.

I don't think I have ever seen her up on the cliff.

I had seen Pops up there though. He would go up to fix things for Mrs. Bertram. I saw him up there, one evening, right on the edge of the cliff looking out to sea. His body looked so small, so far from me. Billowing to be set free.

Silhouetted by the sun, I drew the craggy line of the cliff all the way up to him, pointing my finger. When I got up to him my small finger completely blotted him out of view.

I was more like Pops than Maman, disappearing like that. I watched and listened more than playing a part. I listened even when I shouldn't be listening. If you are still and quiet enough people and animals forget you are there. And the only reason you know you are there is because what you hear thrills.

Here I am now, looking down at things and all the connections I make. The connections I'm making in my head, that is. Me and

Bunny. Two magnets pulling together in two different drawers, I could feel him. But when we were together, a strange loneliness came over me. I didn't read into his silences like I did with other people. Occasionally I would ask him what he was thinking about. Often he would laugh and say, "I don't even know Rozel I was just looking out to sea." Then he would stroke my hand or touch the end of my finger with his without taking his gaze off the water.

I felt safe that he was who he was. That he had no holes and no walls to him. Uncomplicated in a striking way like a bird swooping or a fish jumping. When he looked at me, I would be able to see right to the bottom of the pool, without a ripple. I would fall down to the stillness, where the clearness of the water stopped in time.

He's as messy as the common. His face isn't the kept lawns of the gardens sat on the big cliff. He's wild ground where the weather can play. He's the cliff against the sea air. I love to look at him when he doesn't notice. I'd be bored with a beautiful face. Look at his shallow water cove eyes and the light that moves across it, his face like a hapless seal breaking the surface of the water. My mind jumps from his face across time and memory, and back again to him. In less time than it takes to blink.

The sea today reminds me of the wash bowl, the pattern of blue standing stuck on a plate. In the middle of the plate, the sun painted with its fan of colourful rays. I had to lift up the blue sea bowl to see it complete, otherwise it was always partly hidden by the blue above. I'd lift it thinking I was the strongest tide, lifting the whole sea up til it was sky.

Aunt Sylvie had the sun bowl and the blue plate and Maman had the blue bowl and the sun plate. I don't know but I'm guessing they took half of a pair each. The image of the plates and bowls took me to a memory of the time at my birthday lunch, Maman made the biggest sponge cake, the cake fell on the floor and all the dogs rushed in and ate the whole lot before we could pick any up from under the upturned sun plate they were nuzzling their noses under. I chuckled to myself thinking about it. Bunny looked out to where I was facing, to see what had made me laugh. Inside and outside worlds confused. The moment between us, disjointed, me just shrugging like I didn't know where the giggle came from.

When you become close to someone, they still don't have the key to everything that goes on in your head. Even if you lived together forever, there's always that second life of thoughts that you will never share. My head has more world than the world can hold.

Chapter 24

Just when I thought I knew exactly where I was in life, Bunny surprised me. He turned to me and from nowhere up on the tower, he blurted.

"I want to marry you one day, Rozel."

He said it without a stutter and in a steady block by block way that made me think he had practised it.

I looked out to sea. He wasn't asking me for an answer, at least I don't think so, he was just saying what he wanted, so I just kept on looking out to sea. My mind didn't have a single thought to share with him. I felt like I was going way too fast on my bike, in a rush of bumps and the fear of falling off. I turned to him, raised my eyebrows and we both laughed at my answer.

When I want to say "I love you" to someone I really love, I don't want to find a better way, I just want them to know I mean it. Simplicity is pure. Maman says, "To say something simply with heart, is always what real artists are striving for."

I'd look at the pictures in the big art book we have that lives on the side table in the living room. It's of some of the artists who have pictures in the Louvre, which is a big art gallery in Paris. They were in three categories: portrait, still life, and then landscape. Flicking the glossy pages and brushing the pictures with my fingertips (which I am pretty sure you can't do in the actual place) I'd think, "Why would an artist paint a bowl of fruit instead of a face?" I mean, what could they be trying to say about an apple that they could not say in a face? A bowl of apples sitting on a tablecloth in a room. What could be more normal? But then Maman would say, "Look at the different brush strokes of the different artists, Rozel. Look how they make that apple real. See the fruit is shiny and new here or about to rot here. This is still life. Captured." And she would tut and say, "Oh la la" and sigh and look at the picture again.

Is that why we look at art? To see ourselves better? Is that why Bunny and I come up here so we can look down below us at still life?

Today our life was not standing still, not with Bunny and his talking a future we couldn't know.

He'd read my silence as a future yes. We all say yes before we know, don't we? As Maman said, "This isn't a rehearsal, Rozel; if it was, we would do everything better."

Bunny was looking out to sea smiling.

Just then I heard shuffling of feet coming up the steps towards us. Some people we didn't know, tourists probably, popped their heads up into the daylight of the open roof and said, "Hello." We said a quiet hello back.

They stood to look at the view, pointing out all the places they could see and where they had walked from. We sat with our backs against the wall, listening to them talk about things they knew nothing about. Talking about the bay like they had discovered it themselves.

When they had finished, they turned and smiled at us as though it was our tower and went back down as quick as they had come up.

Chapter 25

I spent more time at Bunny's house up on the cliff now and soon became part of the comings and goings.

Our cottage had more ebb and flow than Bunny's, I suppose there's more than double of us to come and go. Mrs. Bertram has fewer places to go than Maman what with her shopping, her working, her sisters. I don't know who Mrs. Bertram even knows to visit, but she takes herself out to run an errand and then later, another, spacing them out. If it was me, I would have done them all in one go so I could get back up here in peace.

Bunny's room was stopped in time, all the young him was still laid out, though he had made attempts to shelf them. He had a whole army of tin soldiers held down by their feet on an oval coin of metal, that steadied their action poses. A box with a train on the front presumably holding the train pictured leaned against the end of the bed. High on his wardrobe, behind the wooden façade, I could see the edges of a teddy bear, its round foot like the moon behind a cliff. He'd pushed it back enough to hide it from visitors but even in its dusty state, I could see it had been loved to bald fur.

I was in the corridor on my way to the bathroom and couldn't help but look into the doorway of Mrs. Bertram's room. I wondered if her room would give away her dreams or the things I didn't know about her, like Maman's room.

Surely a room that you sleep in is the corridor to the rooms of what we don't say.

I sidled into the room, taking gentle steps, my heart loud in my throat. It was a small, white painted squarish room. Ahead of the door and a few steps from the end of the bed was a deep box window, jutting out past the walls into the sky. Two slim windows joined by a picture window split it into three. The smaller windows were sash opening with a small brass half bowl clasp sitting on top of the gloss white wood frames like tiny crowns. Yellow cotton curtains butter-cupped the white of the paintwork with their golden letting in of light. The sunlight directly through from the windows (without the curtains to yellow it), painted broad dazzling white lines down the walls and onto the floor. The glass in the windows gone, forgotten for the pull of the huge sky behind them.

The sky is all grey with white clouds piled up on top of each other like towels on a shelf, from the horizon to the top of the sill. Only a ruler's width at the bottom of the frame shows the cliff's ground. I'm sure if Mrs. Bertram lay in bed, she wouldn't see the ground floor and she could imagine she lived in the clouds.

It was a similar bed frame to Maman's and Pops'. A black, metal, hollow tube frame. Hers had more simple bends, less finials and decoration than Maman's. Straight black lines held on to each other with simple grip fists of metal joining. It was flat with a blanket instead of a bulky bedspread, with greys and yellows weaving in and out until they became a knotted mix at a fringe of either end.

The room had a peace to it, as I stood taking it in, the air felt soft and fresh like soap. The picture on the wall was a view of the bay, a sailing boat with pink sails almost at shore. Were they pink material or pinked by the light? The sky in the picture had been stained over time, a lukewarm tea colour poured over the clouds, taking the time of the day away from the picture and stealing its glow. Dabs of paint were brushed all over the sea in light and dark shades, the depths below and the reflecting sky above. I imagined sitting down as the artist and using the paint and the brushes to become the sea, from my mind and through my arm to touch the canvas. How strange that Mrs. Bertram chose to hang a picture on her wall of the sea, when the window had the real living thing. Had the picture toned down its colours in jealousy? The rug underneath the window had been saved from the fading bleach of the sun. It was singing in garish reds with interlocking orange squares and diamonds all the way to the shadow of the wall. Its happiness was flat and open like Bunny's face looking at the sea. I wanted to sit on the bed, but decided that wouldn't be a good idea. At home I like to sit in a chair where someone else usually sits. Maman curses me if she sees me copying a walk or a smile or a way of talking; she thinks I am making fun of someone or being mean. But I do it to try and live in the body of someone else. I feel the same here now in her room.

I look out of the window and I am her, thinking her thoughts into her sky.

When you sleep alone in a bed, I suppose both sides can be your favourite side. You can take turns to even out the bed. You could get out on the far side of the bed, though I have no idea why you would.

On the side table, a shallow, empty bowl. How strange to have nothing in it. I skated my finger from one side to the other sliding it down into the shallow curve and up the other side. Slipping over the small pretty flowers under the iced glaze. I put my hand in a fist and saw that my whole hand could fit in the bowl.

It was empty and now it is full.

Only I would know I had been in her room, mapping it out.

Is this the person I might become?

Just then, I heard Mrs. Bertram's footsteps at the bottom of the stairs and I quietly moved back towards Bunny's room.

Once I found a toy car under the chair in our living room. It was right at the back in the corner. It was covered in that strange hairy dust that collects under chairs. I mean, where does that stuff come from? It was a silvery sky blue car, like the cars in American films. Although it was small, the doors opened and closed with a satisfying click and you could peer right in or put your finger into the driving seat. This was the one toy that all three brothers wanted all the time. I longed to hold it, play with it but it was always in one of their hands or in a pocket or parked by one of their plates on the table at dinner. One Christmas they all got a red car, each car was slightly different so they could tell theirs apart from the others. Just like that, the blue car was forgotten. We didn't see it again. No one had noticed it had gone, no one looked for it. Just like that, the red cars were the new babies now.

Poor John, I thought. The blue car lost.

A scratching sound in the eaves broke my thought. Birds nesting in the walls, in the gap between inside and out.

Chapter 26

John came into the kitchen. He put his arms around me.

"My lovely Rozel, she always knows what I'm saying, don't you?" He was hugging me and talking soft and kind and it felt good. When John was like this it was like walking your dog. Tail wagging, stepping together looking out for each other.

"I saw Bunny tonight, I was asking him what's he going to do with himself, you know, in the future. He said he might go travelling! See the world!"

John said this close to my face, searching my eyes. My heart was banging and I swear John could see it beating out from my chest, under my jumper.

"He can do what he wants, can't he?" I replied as nonchalantly as I could.

"I bet Bunny will miss the tower and all its 'views'," said John, putting his arm around me again.

My blood was cooking so hard now, chattering the lid.

"Why are you talking about the tower?" I turned and looked at him, the blush creeping up my neck.

John smiled a slow grin that lifted up and over the horizon line of his lips, pulling nearer to his nose. He had hooked me in. He'd felt the tug of the line and he was just there waiting for a bite. I looked down at the flagstones. I'm the dog fish, kicked in the stomach.

"How long have you known we meet up there?" I added to the floor.

"I saw you a couple of months ago on the top together," he said laughing.

"You spying?"

That's all I said.

John's warmth blew cold without any warning. The dog was snarling now not wagging its tail.

"Do *you* think you are so special that I would go out of my way to find you? Oh, your life interests me so much. Special Rozel. Like I have nothing else in my life but to spy on you?" He spat out the word spy and I saw globules of spit pass and arc over my shoulders. "No, you little idiot. Maybe Bunny can't keep a secret for you? He wanted to tell me all of it."

"Liar." I cried.

I ran to my bed, cried into the pillow with thoughts that wouldn't think straight. John twisting threads of what he knew, into a ball, and I couldn't untangle it. I got up and sat at the top of the stairs watching John.

John was sitting at the table. His triumphant smile had left him. The fuel of his unkindness to me had burnt up. He'd let his temper go again.

John was thinking and then looked at me and said, "That decrepit Mr. Willow shouted over to Bunny the other day. He said, 'You like the tower as much as you like Rozel!' with his sandpaper voice."

John then said he had watched Bunny turn, mutter "idiot" under his breath and walk away.

"So I wasn't spying. Well, not on you anyway!"

I saw John rub at his hair. Everything was coming at him these days. Being in the hole alone, to now when someone was always watching him.

My head hurt. John needed to lie down. I can feel the tipping back, the start of a seizure in John. They say dogs can smell a seizure before it happens. I always feel like the room goes hotter and I get that sick feeling where your stomach lifts up to touch your heart. If I could get him to bed before it happened, sleep might come first and soften his shaking brain.

"John," I came down the stairs and whispered. "It's going to happen soon, get up to bed."

He stood up, staggered to the stairs and managed to make it to his room before the shaking began. I put a heavy blanket over him and watched as he shook uncontrollably. His eyes wild, stuck inside the rocky ride. It slowed and stopped and I put him on his side, kissed him on the forehead, felt him heavy and tired out on his pillow and quietly I closed the door. I lay still for a long time on my bed thinking of John. What it would feel like to be the winner and the loser. To be the fastest and then the slowest.

I got up and out early.

The stairs of the tower felt damp, as always, but it was just their old cold grabbing at my body heat. The sunlight never got round the corner of the tower and up this far. The cold in here was probably as old as the tower. I sat there waiting for Bunny feeling that same cold stone seep up into my sitting bones and silence my muscles. I rubbed at my knees, for warmth, with the palm of my hands and felt the perfect match of my cupped hand to the ball of my knee.

I heard him at the bottom before he even got to the entrance. His footsteps getting faster towards me. My thoughts were frowning my face and when Bunny turned up into my view he looked surprised at me.

"Rozel. Are you okay?"

"John said things to me about you."

I looked at his face. It had fallen just like mine and he was in the old cold tower stone shade just like me.

"Come," he said and took my hand to stand me up. He led me up to the far end of the tower and into the sunlight. This was his answer to me, but then he carried it on with words. "Was it about travelling? Because you know what I said to him, it was about being free. We both talked about it. I don't want to be trapped and neither does he. He wants to be free from the house, from his legs. I'm from this island but I don't want to be here because of that. All the things laid out for me are here, but what about the things I don't even know?"

As he said it his arms were swimming outwards like he was laying it all in front of me.

"Why take just this as the only place, the only way to live? But when I said all that to him, I imagine I am with you, exploring together." He lifted my hand in his and stretched it out towards the horizon. "But I would never say all that to John if he hadn't asked first, if he hadn't known!"

He looked at me.

"John knows about us, about the tower. He said Mr. Willow told him about us."

"Mr. Willow said something to me when John was there, but

he'd got at John too and said other stuff to him asking him if he knew about our hiding place." Bunny was shouting against the wind angrily. "He's twisted, that man," said Bunny, not seeing the picture of a twisted willow he had made in my head. "My mum says keep away from him, but he's the one that creeps up and says things to us children. He's the one that seems to know everything that goes on. Like he's everywhere. And everyone puts up with him because he's so creepy that he must be okay or something. I mean why does everyone put up with him?"

Then he shrugged and said, "Well, what else does he do with his life except watch and wait? He sets traps for the rabbits, eats the song birds that come into his garden and now he's moved on to humans.

"In some ways he and John are the same. They both like to trap things but really they are the ones trapped. "

I'd never heard Bunny talk about people before in this way. He was looking at the sky and looking into people's lives and making decisions about them from thin air.

"I mean, why does John even care about us being together anyway?" Bunny said.

"Our secret is gone," I said.

"But Rozel, we are still here," he said and hugged me.

The tower breathed in then out and the ground it was on, gave, like a pillow letting, and we sank into the moment with soft release.

Chapter 27

Mr. Willow's horse, the one with huge hairy feet that pulled his trap, had her foal last week. The brothers and I went to see it come into the world. First there was one horse in the stable with the new hay all laid out fresh and golden and then we saw two hooves under her tail poking out. Stone solid pieces of bones hanging half in and half out of her body. I winced and my buttocks clenched and tightened at the sight. The legs were working their way further all the way till we could see the back of its body. A wet tail slapped out and then stretching out further came the whole foal until, like dropping a jelly fish back down onto the sand, it unfolded, crash landing into the world. The horse, with blood and stuff dangling out from its behind was pushing and nudging the baby foal with its nose and getting it onto its feet. It was still wet and glossy, as it wobbled onto its legs with the white streaks of birth fluid painted on it, more like a seal than a horse with its wet pelt.

As clear as a bell it rang in my head. "Creation!"

There is a new thing alive that wasn't there before! It was simple conclusion but felt like a huge cartwheel of a thought. There was one horse here and now there are two.

I put my tongue to the top inside of my mouth and felt the wetness and the rough hard arc of the roof of my mouth. I licked around my cheeks with my tongue, seeing if I could remember what it was to be inside a body like that baby foal had just been.

It had stood up and its spindly legs with their bulbous knees shaking and shivering planted down first steps. Its body looking far too heavy for those legs that not five minutes before had been folded inside the belly of its mum. But look now! Here it was alive, a replica, a prize at the end of a Russian doll. I found myself clapping, tears from my eyes dripping down onto the shoulder of my dress.

Even the brothers were quiet after the scene, which I thought was weird because there was lots of describing of disgusting stuff that happened they could have talked about. But I guess the magic of birth got to them too.

The mother horse was breathing hard. Her chest was rising up and then sucking in hard, showing her ribs. She made whinny noises like she was trying to get more air into her body. We didn't know if that was normal after what she had just achieved.

It turned out it wasn't. Two days later we heard the news and saw Mr. Willow crying to himself while digging a huge hole for his beloved horse. As long as I had known Mr. Willow, he had owned that horse.

In the coldest winter, I had seen him guide it in, up the steps and through his front door, hay down in the living room, the fire on for them both.

"Nothing but good that horse," he said to himself as we looked on. It had been the closest thing to a wife that man had ever had. Here we were stood watching the next chapter from where we had stood a few days before watching a miracle.

"Poor baby needs adopting." He had said to the dead body as if it could still hear and understand.

Mr. Willow's horse didn't look dead to me. Its coat was the same dark colour, not paler or shrunken. It lay still on its side on a huge blue tarpaulin as if sleeping on a blanket. But as I looked closer at its face, its lip was set back so you could see its gums, its teeth baring dry in the air.

Pops had taken all the ivy off the side of the cottage one year to stop it getting into the spaces between the stone and ruining the building. That's all I could think of looking at the horse's face, a bare wall of teeth.

He had dug the hole for the horse just past the garden wall, at the start of the field where we usually saw it. Square tiles of turf were piled up in a tower to be laid back over once he'd filled the hole in. The flat rug of its body, now close to the edge of the hole. Mr. Willow had put the cloth underneath it to pull it across and into the grave. The sound of his shovel going into the ground, chipping a bigger hole had a rhythm to it, clockwork tick. He worked tirelessly, his arms, bare as he took layers off from the heat of the work. No one helped. This was his work of love. We stood quietly watching. The brothers were sitting on the fence, I leant my head on my hands, propping my elbows on the fence post. Mr. Willow's mechanical and tireless way of digging meant before long he was in a huge mud bowl of a grave and standing straight for the first time, instead of bent digging, pulled the wooden ladder down from the flat side and climbed out.

He'd wiped his face with muddy hands and I could see tear mark lines run through his dirty cheeks where he had been crying in the hole. He looked over at us and waved. John stood next to me, elbowed me to leave with him, then turned and walked away.

No one waved back to Mr. Willow.

He didn't react to us not waving, just got back to his job, walked towards the horse throwing the spade down hard into the grass so it speared in and remained upright. Then he started to pull the tarp closer to the hole. The horse barely moved in its dead weight, and the tarp pulling so tight.

I left before the horse went in the ground. I just couldn't bear to see the soil go over its head. Frank and David stayed. I think David would have come with me but didn't want to leave Frank there on his own. I can't imagine David enjoying watching the burial. He was such a sensitive soul, but had been the complicit viewer of much cruelty instigated by John and Frank over the years.

It wasn't planting a bulb, for something to grow. That horse wanted to be in the fields on its legs, like it used to, taking its time to walk to all four corners of the field. It wanted to be linking its neck over the side of the wall and grabbing at the longer juicier green grass beyond its confines. It wanted to shake its head, side to side, shaking its mane into rippling fringes like the ones around the bottom of the red lamps at the Smugglers. Vibrate its lips together in front of its stonewall of teeth. It was inside something once, waiting to be born.

Now it was flat, a cut out of something living, its eyes were windows with the curtains closed. The hollow that used to be a horse was in that dark damp hole to be covered up. Had it only been a few days ago, we had seen the foal come out of that living horse and turned one into two? Now only one horse.

I walked up the cliff, leaving David and Frank watching Mr. Willow doing the pulling work that the horse had done for him for so many years. The horse had been his only family, his longest companion.

The foal was too young to work and needed milk from a surrogate mother, so was taken away to another farm.

The foal had gone that morning to a farm on the next cove with a horse that was heavily pregnant. It was already producing milk for the new foal to have. But the foal just wouldn't bond to the horse. It wouldn't take the milk offered to it. It wandered to the lower fields as if looking for its own mother. Searching for something that was gone, it was pulling at the ground with its feet to find its own soil.

It got thinner and weaker, pining and braying. Something had to be done.

The ground was still fresh in squares of turf on top of the grave when Mr. Willow decided to dig his horse back up.

The brothers were back at the same place at the front of the fence.

"The best tickets in the show," Frank said darkly.

Pops had offered to help Mr. Willow once he'd heard about what he was planning. Mr. Willow had said no to Pops and everyone else's help. The horse had been his only family and even standing to watch him dig it up again felt like an intrusion into a private chore. So little happened on the island that this strange, sad moment was the equivalent to us as the circus coming to town.

What Mr. Willow did next is still the strangest of things I've ever seen.

Once Maman put her coat on really quickly to nip out of the kitchen to get some eggs when it was raining and she somehow got her arm stuck elbow first in the seam and she struggled, tugging to free her arm by herself. Her trying to get out of that coat was the nearest thing to what Mr. Willow was doing now.

Other things that it reminded me of, cutting out a bad bit of potato, or peeling a dried and once wet face cloth that had hung on the side of the bath off to wet the stiff shape out of it. The hooked moment of what he did was all those things.

Mr. Willow was looking smaller in the hole with the big dead horse, who, despite being in the ground a week still looked like a horse. The darkness of its coat was repelling the clagging soil. Mr.

Willow in his long green wading boots was straddling that horse with his feet on either side. From here it looked like someone had told him the wrong way to ride a horse. He was sat with his legs astride the horse's belly, side on. It looked ridiculous and comical. But no one was laughing.

He reached behind him and pulled out of the back of his trouser top a long knife. The handle had been hooked into a loop by his belt and the knife itself had been hidden under the tweedy brown, so it felt like a magic trick as it appeared.

Its silver was the glint of treasure among all the darkness and the brown of the horse and the hole.

At the base of the horse's neck he made a line, two or three times gentle with the knife as if he was practicing or drawing in his mind first. Then he stuck the sharp end of the knife into its neck. My cheeks went up with my hands, to shield my eyes. I found myself wincing at the solid knife, half in and half out of the soft horse. I felt the pain for it because it was dead and couldn't feel anything for itself.

Mr. Willow pulled down and down, with both hands gripping, zipped the knife to undo the coat of fur from the body and then turned the knife at a right angle and went up and over its belly. It looked like he was drawing a saddle into its skin. What the hell was he doing?

Pops arrived and I looked at him with a scrunched up face that still hadn't relaxed from watching this horror in front of us.

"You want some help there?" Pops shouted to Mr. Willow and at the same time rubbing me on the back.

Mr. Willow shook his head in answer without looking up.

It seemed crazy to watch a frail old man cut a shape in a horse, in a hole; we weren't any part of it except for watching and we had no idea of his plans. The boundaries between him and us were the rules of what he could do and what we could do. In his world he could intrude onto our side any time, in our lives, in our home; but we couldn't do the same. He was our landlord, after all, and we were careful to remember our home was his property. Maybe that's why Pops and Maman were always sticking up for him to us children.

He held everything in his hands. Maman and Pops knew they had to be on his good side.

What Mr. Willow was doing wasn't madness, digging up his dead horse and cutting the skin into a saddle. It was so it could be used to trick the foal into bonding with another horse. The smell of his mother reborn. It had been done before as a way to bond an orphaned animal on the island and had worked. Mr. Willow was saving the foal.

After we had all gone, Pops had stayed to talk and Mr. Willow had shared his plan, and Pops had told Maman and of course Maman talks to all of us and into her soup.

"It must have hurt like hell to see that animal, the one thing he loved come back out of the soil. To then cut at it, pull at the flesh and then stick it back in the ground again, what a thing." Maman had said pulling the brown harder skin off the shallots.

Who could do that and stomach it? I thought. When someone dies, people say rest in peace, and seeing the re-wake that went on that day, I can understand why. After he cut out the rug off the horse's back, the soil filled the hole over and the cut out piece was taken to the farm with the new foal and it went onto the new mum horse like a blanket over its back.

I will never ever complain about a hand me down winter coat again.

A live horse walking round with a dead horse saddle.

I felt sick at the thought.

The plan worked, though. The foal took to the new horse and started to feed, putting on weight and strength in leaps and bounds. A bond was formed. The clever, practical, disgusting plan worked and people talked about it at the Smugglers, Pops said, saying it was a selfless act of Mr. Willow's to try and save the foal.

The dead horse was back in the ground with its bare flesh saddle open and ready for worms and rot to set in. The hole was filled again and tramped down with Mr. Willow's shuffling feet, a flamenco dance, flattening jig, making sure this was the last time the horse minus its skin would be out in the fresh air. This was the final act of the show that we watched by the fence.

Chapter 28

Normal things happened. Pops was at the Smugglers, of course he was.

The seagulls circled the boats as they came back in the morning. The sun made it once again over the cliff and warmed up the common. The kitchen was steaming with another pot on the stove.

Then Maman got a call from the local doctor.

He had been sent to see Mr. Willow and then another doctor and another, the news was not good.

Mr. Willow was bed bound, for the foreseeable future. There was a budget set to have someone visit daily and care for him at home. Mr. Willow had requested he stay home instead of hospital to the doctor and it had been agreed that the doctor could arrange visits and someone could check on him daily, bring his food. Being his closest neighbours, we were the doctor's first port of call. The fee was the same as two hours of Maman's cleaning job and "The extra money would help with all the outgoings of our growing family," Maman had said when Pops had shaken his head.

Pops rarely gave his opinion and rarely disagreed with Maman in front of us.

"It wouldn't be much to do," said Maman. "A bit of food and helping with the toilet and checking on him, that could be easily done between us."

Looking at Pops. By us she meant me and her.

It was expected, this frailty of Mr. Willow what with his age, the doctor had said. But the doctor couldn't understand the speed of this decline. Old age didn't come with these fevers and convulsions and the rattling, in his chest like an animal in a cage. Mr. Willow's body and mind had been slowing down in his old age said the doctor, all life when you get old is up hill. This wasn't slow and steady, not a gentle pressing of the brake. This was an emergency stop.

The doctor had sent off his blood for tests, but he said, until the results came, to be better safe than sorry. Under no circumstance were we to touch him (as if that was my plan) without washing our hands straight away before and after. Mr. Willow's life had been pruned back and confined to one room.

I realised now that I hadn't seen him for most of the summer. I hadn't thought about him or missed waving at the window. His cart hadn't clattered over the rocks on the path, sounding like shivered teeth since his horse had died. Looking back, I hadn't seen him since the last horse burial; maybe that is why those weeks and days felt long and free.

He owned this place and now he was missing, it was our world.

Maman sat me down and said we could share the money and the responsibility of the job, if I wanted. She didn't know how long we would have to keep going and this way we could make sure there was one of us able to do it if the other couldn't. Of course I said yes — who can say no to Maman. I didn't relish the idea of spending time in his house on my own. I had avoided it all my life, except that one time when I'd knocked at the front door to go in, and that had been for John. I'm sure I could do it again for Maman.

The doctor had left us a key ring in a big brown envelope labelled 'Mr. Willow's KEYS'. The word 'keys' was underlined three times and much bigger than his name. The first and biggest key was the heavy mortice for the front door. Its weight pulled Maman's apron pocket downwards and the hem fell further that side, stretching the stitches. Behind the front door key in a queue on the ring, the back door key, the wood store key, two keys that looked like suitcase keys and three more door keys unknown.

"So many keys we don't need on here but we'll carry them anyway, it means the ones we need are easier to find," said Maman laughing, pretending that the bunch were too heavy to hold.

"Let me know, if you think of anything Mr. Willow's done different recently," said the doctor. "Has he travelled abroad?" he asked as he started to move sideways away from us. "It may be some foreign bug."

He said the word foreign like it was a swear. I didn't like him.

Thinking of Mr. Willow anywhere in the world except the cove felt as unlikely as the sun swimming in the sea.

"You'll only need the first one," said the doctor, meaning the big key, as he left. "Call me if you think he is worsening or if there is any change. I will be coming regularly anyway."

"What did he mean by that? How can we tell?" I had asked Maman after she had shut the door behind the doctor.

"We will know," said Maman solidly. She had seen enough people she knew go from this side to the next. "Tell you what, let's go now, Rozel, then the rest of the day is free." Maman started putting on her coat.

I wasn't ready.

But, I put my coat on too. Off we both went towards his big house, too big for just him.

"Have you known him all your life, like me?" I asked Maman.

"I was thinking just the same the other day," she said looking at me and smiling. "He's been here as long as I have. But I don't think I have ever really known him."

She said it looking up as if the answer might have been above the door, out of reach. She opened the front door and it creaked into the darkness of the hallway. The smell of cold stale air told us no-one had been downstairs in the house for a while.

"Go and put the kettle on, Rozel," Maman said, kicking the envelope forwards from the door.

I walked ahead to the kitchen, Maman climbed the stairs to see what state Mr. Willow was in before I got there. I was thankful of that.

Filling the kettle in the kitchen, the smell of things growing and rotting had an unpleasant sweetness like Mr. Willow's smile. "I don't want to be on my own here," I said to myself. I kept looking behind me, my heart jumping at nothing but the creaks from upstairs.

I opened the small window by the kettle, taking the dirt from the sill onto my fingertips and leaving clean little dots behind. The fresh air diluted the stale smell a little and I opened the kitchen door, then walked up the stairs.

If the smell in the kitchen was cloying, his bedroom was worse.

It smelled of green garden ponds, damp moss like the kitchen but there was something else, a red smell, different, darker, like rotting flesh. It smelled of caves, of earth, of birth and of tin. The metallic stuck at the back of my throat and nose.

The time in his room was stuttering silence, with a slow decay. I was as impatient as the patient seemed serene. Every inch of me desperate to leave. He had taken this room, out of the four upstairs, as his bedroom. The west facing corner, that looked out from the front of the house, over towards our cottage, with a postage stamp sized corner of the bay and sea visible in the bottom of the window. Going to get an extra blanket for Maman, I noticed the other rooms upstairs were dressed up as bedrooms with different candy-coloured thick candlewick covers over the beds. The dust that lay on them told how little they were used. What had been whitewashed stone walls were darkening with a grey mould. The corners of the ceilings were darkest, like night shadows had been trapped by cobwebs. I noticed how decay travelled along the edges and corners like a distrusting cat, sticking to the blind spots, behind furniture. It conquered a corner, doubling in size while nobody watched, drip by drip.

Walking to the window, after giving Maman the blanket, each of my footsteps were too loud and wooden. I was slapping into the quiet of the room, Maman put her finger to her lips, and I nodded, lifting back the dirty net curtain to one side between the least of my fingertips, looked out from the speckled eggshell glass.

The mould had grown through onto the window, the net curtain patterns of large blousy flowers in rows now green and black. I picked a tissue out of my pocket and wiped an arc.

It was a brush stroke of daylight that streamed into that arc like a rainbow of bright, out at the view.

I could see right over towards our cottage.

To see your own world from a different place is so strange.

Our cottage looked so small and plain. It was hard to imagine how we all fitted into the squat square building below the roof.

Framed in the distance, through this dirty window, the magic I felt when I was in the warm nest of our family, was gone.

I heard a murmur behind me.

I turned my head towards the bed.

The framework of Mr. Willow was sleeping in his bed.

How much of him inside was still awake or alive?

The bedspread arched up and over him like the hill down into the cove.

Like the hill with all the things buried underneath.

If John was the hole, Mr. Willow was the hill.

Maman was puffing up his pillows, with her soft hands, asking him if he was okay, if he wanted a drink. She was gentle and firm at the same time, a natural control. Mr. Willow was smiling a distant smile. He was nodding at everything Maman was asking and that made it more confusing, what he wanted, so Maman just answered for him.

I heard the kettle and went down to make tea. The smell had gone a little in the kitchen so I closed the window. After tea, Maman said, we should clear out the cupboards of the sprouting vegetables, so the kitchen won't smell so bad. The potatoes were looking like spider crabs with their tubes of white reaching out to seed themselves. How things grow from one thing to another! The shape of a round potato, then from nowhere huge arms grow, but where were those arms hiding in there? From tadpoles to green legs, black dots to jumping frogs. Maman had gone back up to check on him, came down the stairs quietly carrying a plate and a cup and a towel. The first thing she did was wash her hands even though the bar of soap was a cracked piece of driftwood stuck to the soap dish.

We wiped down all the brown rotting carrot stains in the cupboards, swept the dirt that had fallen off the leeks. Cleaned out everything in there to stop mice from getting a hold of the kitchen without a human or cat paw to stop them. We had washed out the milk bottles, scrubbing the thick, cheese halo rings inside with a toothbrush. The front step was full of them, ready to be collected, by the time we had finished. A little crowd of glass people full of fresh air. We washed our hands again and again, shouted up the stairs we were going, then we left.

Each day since then, Maman and I have come, sometimes together, but mostly taking turns so we both get a break from it.

The time always slows in his room, especially when I am there on my own — well, he is there, but I wish he wasn't. There is no clock upstairs, but at the bottom of the stairs, in the hall, is an old French grandmother clock.

"Slightly shorter than a grandfather clock," Maman says, as if to explain the difference. "And with an open casing showing the big brass pendulum, just like my grandmother."

One of our jobs before dealing with Mr. Willow, is to wind the clock. It needs two half turns with the key that sits by the plates on the architrave above the face.

The key looks like a cartoon windup toy key with a small cylindrical hollow tube leading to a flat large head end with three semi circles intertwined.

There were strict instructions left in writing that this must be done each day as the clock had been with the Willow family for centuries and had never been allowed to stop. I'm not sure if the letter with instructions had been left out for us and written by Mr. Willow, or they were instructions given for him to use.

If he died, where would this clock go? Mr. Willow had no family as far as I knew, and I wasn't sure where the instructions in the letter had come from. Who becomes the caretaker of what we leave behind?

Winding the clock up was a solid job. You turned the key and the clock kept ticking. There was little else that had such a satisfying result. Mr. Willow hardly noticed us there. Keep him clean, feed him, keep him ticking.

He is in a mind world of his own.

We are getting strange glimpses of what he is seeing and talking to.

He was fretting about falling out of the cart yesterday, too near the cliff. Upright in his bed.

"If I fall down I'll never get up. I can't make it up the sides" he said. Then he looked the other way as if someone had come into the room, but nobody had, and started to giggle. Giggle like a little child. When he looks, we look too.

"I must fall in," he said, then whispered, "I can't do that."

Maman and I glance at each other and check if we are there together with him, still in the room. A shared moment, then he was gone again. But when I'm there alone, without Maman, his words crept around me.

He was babbling about a silver fish a minute later pointing to a jug on the mantle. The jug was white stoneware with hand painted blue flowers and threads of what seemed like vines around in an even but not uniform fashion. The spout was an ample V for pouring and it had a sturdy wide base, getting wider at the middle and then in slightly at the top. It was a thick, shiny made thing. Not delicate. Solid, it looked like Maman in her summer dresses. Such beauty. I knew he was pointing to the jug. I even looked into the jug filled with cold water just in case there was a fish in there.

"Fish," he said stabbing his finger towards it. "Silver fish."
I did wonder if he was pointing past the jug, to a fish in the chimney, (not another one), but after he shouted out "Jug!" and "Water!"

So I resisted the urge to look up the chimney, mainly because I didn't want my back to him.

I went and got him a glass and filled it with water, thinking he was thirsty but he pushed the cup away from his mouth. His grip on my hand hurt.

After, it seemed that the effort of being outside of his own head had exhausted him.

His breathing had hollowed out his cheeks, pulling them in past his bones and he was rocking his head side to side on the pillow like a baby avoiding a spoon.

I got all the things together to take to the kitchen before leaving, I heard him mumble some nonsense, then whisper, "I threw him a sandwich so he would stay alive."

Chapter 29

It had been two weeks of Maman and I caring for Mr. Willow, but the times I went alone felt like years.

The blood results were back. Maman said that humans could get a rare disease from digging up dead horses.

"Anthrax," she whispered, like you could catch it from saying it aloud.

He could easily die from it and it was attacking him from the inside out. Making him hollow and unworldly and very fragile.

His delirium had increased with each visit. The doctor said that was to be expected as the toxins were not being cleared from his kidneys and were starting to travel up his body. We were told to try and get water into him even if only with a sponge by his mouth. His mouth was cracked dry and his tongue looked like the sandy beach in summer. When the rock pools dry up in summer, there is always a dip or a shell that can hold the smallest drop of water in that creatures clamp on to survive. But here was Mr. Willow drying out like a cuttlefish for bird food and the drops of water we got into him seemed to disappear. He was pale, leaning against the bars of his bed and his words were sharper edged and cut at his dry mouth as they came out. He now spoke a strange language as his mouth, lost of spit, tried to shape words out past his dry lips. He sometimes sounded like John after the hole — though I could understand what they both said, John had always made sense. Mr. Willow was desiccating, his skin was peeling off in layers of sun-dried flaking sea salt.

He had started to be sick, as his body tried to purge but the sick was black bile. It would gather at the edges of his mouth like he had been sucking on a broken pen. Pooling like the shadowing mould in the corners of the room. Dark circles under his eyes caught the same colour, lined around his mouth.

I would have to wash the bile down the sink from the white washing dish that he would cough into. The contrast and the cough would create a pattern, a little ink splat that I would try and find a picture in. Just like I would look for animals in the passing clouds.

But I hated turning my back on him and I wished that Maman had more time so she could be with me to visit because the hours of dread before it, didn't relieve when I was here.

But I had to turn my back on him to walk away.

As I was taking the bowl away Mr. Willow smacked his lips together and said, "That is my soul there!" Getting louder. "Wash it away. Fade it to grey. Get it out of here."

With each staccato phrase he became more agitated. A skipping song, keeping time. It sang out , louder than his usual mumblings.

"Why are you here?' he said looking behind me.

I turned around to see who he was talking to. How easily another's madness can enter as a truth into us.

"You can't be here," he said again. "I let you die."

Was there someone behind me that I couldn't see? He was so convinced by what he was seeing, he had made me believe it too. A cold creeping at the back of my arm, a finger stroking it, shivering.

There was no one there. Of course there wasn't, I said to myself. I went downstairs and as I touched the bottom step the grandmother clock chimed for five o' clock like I had set it off ringing.

The steps I took on the wood then the stone in the kitchen were singing back what he said.

"You can't be here, I let you die. You can't be here, I let you die."

I could feel my breath, my chest, joining in on the rhythm, running to the well again.

Was Mr. Willow going to rise up from the dead like the frozen soldier?

My head hurt. I felt heavy and tired and the fear in me, pulsing with the seconds on the clock. How much longer did I have to be here? Would Maman be angry if I just left now?

I didn't want to go back upstairs.

I could hear him chatting on quietly to the people only he could see, who kept visiting him. Mr. Willow's madness felt lucid to me. Everything he said sounded more believable than the things he said when he was well. The tone of his voice had truth running through it, his earnest pleadings to these invisibles were a storm cloud of confessions.

It was always raining inside this house.

Even on hot days, the house felt cold. Pops said it was the thickness of the walls but it felt like spirits to me. His head world was acting out a play on every visit. Each time he was giving me pieces of a map, a puzzle, names and places and conversations, and on each short walk back towards the cottage, after the dreaded visits, these things were building into a framework. Was it real and true or feverish lies? Either way, I was seeing things through his eyes and I didn't like it.

As I reached the cottage Maman was waving at the garden gate.

I waved back asking what with my hands, by holding up the sky.

As I got closer she cupped her hands to her mouth and said, "It's a colder night forecast, can you go put this extra blanket on Mr. Willow?"

My heart sank. The light was dimming and I had had my fill of the mould and the silent empty rooms and the noisy madness of his bedroom.

But I took the blanket from Maman and headed back towards his house.

The house was so much taller than ours. It leaned over as you walked up to it. The grey slate roof matched the darkening clouds. They had sponged the dark of the night before the brighter sky behind had a chance.

The windows on the ground floor were all dark, a wall, but the bright landing light shone into the top front two rooms, and those windows had a silver moon glow. I took a deep breath and opened the door.

The scrape of the swollen door onto the quarry tiles made a shrieking sound and I wanted to shush it, for telling on me coming back in the house. I went straight to the stairs, each step shoving my feet forward in a sullen way that felt satisfyingly grumpy. I was doing the right thing for Maman but I could show I didn't want to do it to the stairs.

The bedroom door was open and I could see the pillows and the bedspread. But it was flat and empty. Mr. Willow was not in his bed.

"Where is he?" I mumbled to myself.

He was a hollowed boned baby bird by now. I didn't even know if his legs still worked. Had he flown away?

I looked over at the opposite wall, past the mantle, over in the far corner crouched over and looking at the empty grate, was Mr. Willow. He was a winter tree in a white night dress, looking down at the black grate, his toes on the edge. His eyes were wild and he was throwing something imaginary down at the grate as if it was a hole and then peering in.

"Hello down there!" he said gleefully.

My thoughts stuttered at what I was seeing. My lips dried up like his and the gulp was loud and painful as if I had swallowed a pebble. I was sure my being there would disturb him, I stood there in the doorway as still as I could.

I wanted to see what he was doing and I didn't want to take him out of wherever his crazy head world was right now.

"Hello, Stanley," he said again.

I thought he was there, looking down at a hole, looking down at John. I was so sure he was going to say John's name. Who was Stanley?

"You can't come out. I know you want to and I know you think crying and shouting will help but it won't little one. It won't help you. Crying that way. I'm the only one who knows you're here. No one else. No one else even misses you. Here have a sandwich! Here have a fish!"

Mr. Willow threw down two things into the fire grate hole with his empty hand. I was a witness. But to what?

Mr. Willow turned his head towards me slowly. He locked his eyes onto mine. I couldn't tell if he was in my world or I was in his. But I could feel why the fear, why the skin on my neck prickled with him in the house.

He was uncovered in this moment and there was no doubt. He was dangerous. The creepy unease that I had shrugged off and all the times Maman and Pops had made excuses for him. When I was told by Maman to not listen to gossip, that Mr. Willow was just a strange lonely old man who didn't know how to get on with people.

It had always been there in the driving of his cart.

All of the signs had been so blatant and so true. He had hidden in plain sight as himself, as a wolf while people had dressed him as a sheep. He stared at me, not moving or saying a thing. His eyes unblinking.

"Have you come for John?" he whispered in a song. "Because he's mine now!"

His grey teeth baring a grim smile at me.

I threw the blanket at the bed and ran down the stairs, out the door, past the gate and stopped to look behind me at the sycamore tree. I knew he didn't have the strength to leave the house but I still saw him chasing me. Coming for me, floating in his night dress as a ghost.

Chapter 30

The night sky had darkened. The clouds that had been moving across the light were now gone, losing themselves. Billowing candy floss squeezed until it is nothing but a pill of sugar. The dark felt dizzying. Each step, a dark pool, the hole not there in the grate. Was I going to fall down into it, into the madness?

There was a rage inside me burning like nothing I'd felt before. Blackening my inside to a treacle heart. I didn't want to be taken over by what he had said, to be taken by the darkness. I needed something to get rid of this in me, light and love and something, something. Help me! Help me! Faster, footsteps, faster, faster. Running towards the garden gate, desperate to get there. I didn't want the badness I saw in him to enter into our cottage. The black bile of his soul that he would spit with a ping into the white bowl.

I needed to get it out of me before I got to the door. Before it spread to them too.

I spat and spat his wickedness out onto the bushes in the garden, half sick, snot, saliva, again and again. I rubbed at my arms and down my legs and then combed my fingers through my hair, rubbing my scalp. Get him off me!

At the gate I remembered Maman digging up the box. Precious things can be buried. We hide things because the pain of love gone can't live in the air. She scraped away at the ground that covers up all the things from the past. Her silent shuddering tears fell forward onto the soil as her body turned away, hiding love from us.

When I was gardening with Maman, the first time I had planted potatoes for Pops, I found a spoon while I was digging. The silver glint in the dark made my heart race. I really had found treasure. I went to the sink and ran the water up and down the metal. As I washed off the soil and used the nail brush gently, the water and soap made it shine even more. I started to think of what else was in the garden, brooches, coins, from Egypt, from Rome, treasure to find. I showed it to Pops who exclaimed that it was a stainless steel teaspoon, probably from our drawer, dropped and then accidentally buried.

I kept it anyway.

The truth can be right there to grab but the answer can be taken or left.

Mr. Willow was unravelled. I wanted him to be pulled apart until there was nothing but a pile of string. He had turned our John into a bitter man. Damaged him, not just physically. Left him distrusting the world and everyone in it that became a wall separating him from people, even us. He had never really left the hole and he didn't know what was real or fiction anymore.

He had felt it and Mr. Willow was right over there from him, in the corner of his eye. John was always pushing us away, me, Maman, the brothers, even Pops. But he couldn't push Mr. Willow.

I don't even know if Mr. Willow gave me these secrets or I took them by listening at the door that night.

I was at the gate of our cottage, soon to be inside with them, with his words inside me hiding. I went in. Maman was setting the table. She looked up.

"Was he okay? Was he cold?"

"He was okay," I said.

"So he wasn't cold then?" Maman asked looking back down at the fork she was putting down last. I wasn't even sure how much of an answer she wanted me to give or if she was just rounding off her own phrase.

"He was cold, he was out of bed."

"What?" she said. "He was what?"

"He was out of bed. He was standing and talking strange things, Maman," I said trying to sound at ease.

"He needs to be in bed, Rozel. Tell me you put him to bed," she said looking up at me and pointing with the same one fork left in her hand.

"Yes," I lied. I think it was the first time I had lied to Maman. Directly. About something important. I had left a space other times, when she'd asked me where I had been. When I had secretly been on top of the tower. But I had never directly lied to her. It felt horrid. A tiny black speck of the grate had been inhaled into me and had got lodged somewhere in my chest near my heart.

"Where's John?" I asked, changing the subject.

"He's up in his room," said Maman. "Can you tell him and the brothers it's five minutes til dinner? And I won't be shouting them down more than once."

She huffed, put down the fork, at last, walked towards the pot on the stove. *Bang*. That poor stove.

Maman's way of cooking anything was to cook it for as long as possible regardless of what it was. Oysters in a stew were cooked for at least four hours. Maman thought the longer something was cooked the better it would be. Vegetables would always just about hold their shape in the pan but turn into a puddle when put on the plate. Our ladle was used for almost every meal because almost every meal was made in a pot. A pot cooking on top of the stove, or a pot in the oven. Time was her most used ingredient.

Dinner tonight was in the really heavy black pot with steep sides. It was heavy when it was empty or full and once washed it had to be oiled to stop it from going rusty. It never went into a cupboard because it was rare to have one day without it in use, and no one wanted to bend down to put it away.

I wasn't sure what we were having for tea tonight, it smelt like rabbit stew, but most things Maman cooked did.

What I did like about Maman's cooking was that all the time the pot was on the stove, it filled the cottage with the smell of cooking. It was home. The smell of boiling water, steaming the air has its own perfume. The kitchen's cooking steam and its warm scent comforted me in such a deep, simple way, like everything would be okay.

I put my foot on the first step of our stair and remembered how the clock had chimed in unison with my stepping on Mr. Willow's last step. As if it had been the chimes in A Christmas Carol when the ghosts would arrive. Mr. Willow was like the first and the last ghosts rolled into one. Jacob Marley in his riches gathered alone and the boney arm of death, silent and beckoning.

We didn't have a grandmother clock or a grandfather clock or anything grand for that matter. We didn't have to keep anything ticking or turned for past and future generations. This cottage wasn't ours and we always knew that we were living on Mr. Willow's borrowed time. It should have been ours really. Our lives were planted here, the smells of here smoke-cured into us. Everyone in the bay saw it as ours. But it was Mr. Willow's land.

"Renting is like standing on a rug you own, knowing that at any moment that it could be pulled from under you," said Maman. "Rolled up and gone with every memory of yours folded into it."

She'd said that talking to Sylvie about her move once as I sat by her feet playing with balls of wool. When Mr. Willow had been well, we were safe and secure in the cottage, but who would own it after him?

Our steps were less steep than in Mr. Willow's house. They started further forward in the room and sloped upwards in a graceful way. There wasn't the rock climb of his house. Our banister had so many more hands using it daily, that the wood was shiny and soft and silken, polished by hands alone. Wood can feel its best from slow hand polishing. There is a tree at the bottom of the cliff that everyone grabs as they reach the bottom, and it's like a sash of silk around that one part of it. Just from hands.

Anyway, sliding my hand up the banister, the delicate rubbing against my palm like a touch from our home.

"You going to the bathroom?" Frank shouted as I saw him rush past me, into it and shut the door behind him. He must have thought that was where I was heading. Always grabbing a selfish shot.

David waved his foot out of his bedroom door as he heard me to say hello. His legs stretching past the end of the bed. I shouted hello to him and smiled to myself at his silly warm way.

I went into John's room. He was on the bed threading some new laces into his shoes.

"Snapped today on the common," he said.

I could see the concentration he needed to get each lace into each eyelet, a slow and shaky process.

John was used to his slowness but it was really hard for all of us to not take over and do the task quicker for him. I looked out of his small window to distract myself from my own impatience and how I could have finished lacing by now.

"Maman says dinner in five minutes," I said.

"I heard her from up here," he said, concentrating.

There was a pause from both of us. I think maybe I felt the moment land harder because I knew there was more to say.

"Had to go twice to Mr. Willow's tonight," I said. "Maman made me take a blanket."

"Is he not dead yet?" said John finally pinching the head of the lace with his fingers and through the brass ringed hole.

"Nearly," I said.

"Good," said John.

I felt the need to tell what Mr. Willow had said, rising.

"Did you know anyone called Stanley?" I said.

"What, Stanley from the year above me at school?" John asked sounding confused. "Works on his dad's boat?"

"No, I don't think so," I said. "Doesn't matter".

"Dinner," shouted Maman from downstairs.

"She said she'd only shout it once," I said.

"Dinner," came her voice again.

I put two fingers up. John laughed. He put the finished laced shoe on the floor and left the one to do on his bed.

"Wonder what we are having?' he said.

"Let's guess before she opens the lid," I said.

The cooking was warming me. The family was around me and Mr. Willow was far away from us. I hoped he was freezing, looking down into his hole.

Chapter 31

I was back at the tower. Last night's revelations from Mr. Willow had run around my head, bouncing about and keeping me awake. The chance to speak with John had gone with dinner. I'd come up here to wait for Bunny and as I stood, a whole flock of swans flew overhead. They were honking and arranging themselves into a V. They were flying so low I could see their orange legs and feet tucked up under them. Their wings were making huge flaps and their necks bobbing up and down to counteract the wings' push and pull. A honking shrill like when the door scrapes on the tiles at Mr. Willow's, swans scraping their weight across the sky.

They moved into their V pointing at the distance, still honking. I tipped my head, bending backwards following their flight as they got smaller and smaller, my neck ached and so then I tipped myself back upright so I could turn to look from the other way. When I turned, I couldn't see them at all. It was like they had vanished, in a blink, they were probably just the other side of the cliff or behind some trees. Just because I can't see them doesn't mean they don't exist up there in the sky, but it did feel like a magic trick.

On top of the tower I was part of life in the sky, closer to the birds and inside the clouds. It was a different world to live in, up here. I had never been anywhere but the island and up here in the sky.

There was Bunny.

Down there, all small. Shading his eyes from the sun to look up to the tower.

I waved not knowing if he could see me over the top edge. The pull of the tower as our place was still strong, to be away from the world and just us two. I wanted to tell him about Mr. Willow and all he said last night.

I had asked Maman if she would go that morning to see Mr. Willow instead of me. Maman had agreed but only if I would take him soup at lunchtime. It was a Saturday and I had no work and no other reason to say no to Maman. After all we had both agreed to share the load of caring for Mr. Willow and split it equally.

I never wanted to be in the presence of that twisted bag of bones again. I felt my face scrunch up in disdain, the thought of his face making that happen, here, nowhere near him. I had seen so much of his madness over mine and Maman's visits that I became very aware of myself, questioning my own oddities, of the way I saw the world, which I knew wasn't like everyone else.

I heard Bunny getting closer up the spiral staircase past the wind shell sounds of oceans shushing across the top of the tower.

"A start is always the hardest," says Maman. "The first step, or the first brush stroke."

So I began to talk as soon as Bunny got close and it was like falling. Talking like Mr. Willow, I was acting as him, showing Bunny what it felt like to be me in the room last night. He was looking at me like it was crazy. Piecing together the things I had pieced together. As I said the words Mr. Willow had said I felt the cold, stroking hand of it do the same to Bunny that it had done to me that night.

Then I stopped being Mr. Willow. Which felt really good.

"So what do I do now?" I asked at the end of it all.

"What do you mean what do you do?" said Bunny

"Do I tell anyone?" I said

"You've told me," he said.

"But do I tell John or the brothers or Pops or Maman?" I looked at him for answers.

I let out a huge sigh of air that had been caught up inside me. Bunny was looking confused and kept scraping his bottom lip with his top teeth in his mouth and pulling out. It looked like he was gathering words in his mouth but none came.

He was shaking his head, rubbing his hair and sighing and looking at me.

Finally he said, "Is that who he is though? Is it not the madness? The illness? The thing is people can lose their minds as they get older, Rozel. What if you say all this to someone about him and then it's not true?"

Here it was again. Caution. And the same excuses that Mr. Willow had always been given by everyone.

How must it feel for John trying to work out what the echoes were inside him? Looking to find the bad guy, because he knew in his heart there was one. I just couldn't get them to him. He was reaching out for answers, only finding ghost thoughts.

"Are you there?"

"Are you there?"

It was like John had been asking that for years with his drinking and his moods, the leader knocked out of him.

Poor John.

My heart was weeping for John.

"Are you there?" Bunny was saying to me.

"I'm speaking to the wrong person," I said.

"What do you mean?" said Bunny.

I saw fear in Bunny today, mostly I saw eyes that I thought I recognised from somewhere else.

We looked at each other, me seeing into him. I turned around on him like I had with the flying swans and he disappeared because I didn't look back.

I walked down the stairs. He didn't follow.

Any words left to say to each other, shrank with the distance that I was spiralling between us down the dark stairs and away from him.

No words from him up on the tower down to me on the ground. Caution was caught in his throat. It made me hate him a little, because he reminded me of myself. With the tower behind, I headed for the cottage. I was out of the cold shadow of it and coming for the line of sun.

Chapter 32

Why is it the fragile people, the ones we think will go first, never die? It's always the unexpected, strong and young. Old people can hang on and on, because they have nothing else to do.

Mr. Willow was no bigger from all the soup that we were drowning him with. Every meal we made at the cottage had one extra portion put aside in the enamel bowl to go up to his house. He was the extra guest at every meal.

We had inherited a pet. We fed and looked after him in his mossy rabbit hutch of a huge house, checking his water, his food, cleaning him. Damp sweet hay as you opened the door. All the other rooms in the house were being left to fester and gather dust in their privacy behind pulled shut doors. Maman and I would dust occasionally, sweep, to keep the house where it was but the daily decay of being un-lived in worked its way into the curtains of air and hung limply undrawn.

I had started to wander more out of the main bedroom in between chores, to get away from him.

I couldn't stand hearing his strange inner rants. I hated what I felt and wished when I was with him, willing him to die. I thought it would be the best thing for everybody if he did, like with an old cat that can't clean itself anymore.

It was to keep his dignity. That was how I squared it with myself but really it wasn't for him, it was only for me.

This whole time had been spent with Maman and I, counting days, sharing out the looking after Mr. Willow. I was tired of the rotten routine.

I now woke in the night with vivid dreams accompanied with sweats and shakes and hands grabbing at me. Not the soldier with the sugar coated eyes, it was Mr. Willow with spades for hands, laughing at me down a hole. Or him by my side in the dark night of my dreams, just laughing that awful cackle, him turning his head and the way his eyes locked onto mine, repeated over and over.

He already took up my days, I hated him taking up my nights as well.

His body was shrinking in his bed now and he rarely got up, like the time when he shouted down into the grate. But he was growing in me. I thought about him more than anyone else. He moaned and groaned with pain when I bathed or fed him and it sent me sick. The sounds of him echoed well after I was back home.

His moans had the zingy rubbing finger on a glass rim 'ring' of pleasure when he did it. Long and sonorous. I knew he was in pain, but he chimed as he was taking another step away from this life and its aches.

I would feed him the soup or the stew, spoon by spoon into his dry cave of a mouth and try not to look at him while doing it, while he stared right at me, with unblinking eyes. If I had better, kinder thoughts about him, I could pretend he was a baby owl. A small, weak and helpless animal. His eyes were beady and black, the poisonous bile filling up all the way to the top of his head.

Each spoon he took was so slow. I would get the spoon to his mouth then look out of the window till the dry gulping stopped and then turn back with another spoon. When the bowl was finished, or almost, I would take it down to the kitchen to wash it. That would take no time with a quick rinse and a wipe with the cloth. I would rest it upside down next to the build up of cups on the draining board.

Every day I was there, I did this same routine, wander around the rooms, looking to see this world he had built for himself. Watching and thinking as him. There was a wooden shelf about head height in the kitchen and underneath it he had screwed jam jar lids, so that the jars would screw onto the underside of the shelf and look like they were hanging in mid air. Inside them were various sized screw and nails, bottle tops and small hooks. Separated and sorted into like for like.

On the kitchen table there was a still life scene of three hammers, two frames, a bowl that presumably had held fruit in it and was now empty except for a roll of paper. Just past the table in the corner, around ten to fifteen walking sticks. All of them were wooden with a smooth semi circled hook over the top. Maman had one just like them to grab the juiciest blackberries from the thorny middle of the bushes when we went picking. I had never seen Mr. Willow walk with a stick. Even in this frail state of his now, he didn't use one. Why would he choose to have so many of these in his kitchen?

"An answer can't always be found," said Maman, or was it "An answer can always be found" and I remembered her wrongly? When human nature doesn't have a reason why, how can there be a track back to why? Does he even know why he has them?

Questions are everywhere in this house.

How do you live like this?

Who are you kidding that you sit in this neat tidy room?

Why do you have so many hammers and nails?

Is that what happens when you are alone? Your actions become your conversations with yourself? Distractions are mapped out without anyone to move the things you did, so you see the path. You started fixing a frame then you couldn't find the right screw, you opened a cupboard and then forgot to close it.

I didn't think it was right that I should look in all his closed cupboards, but I itched to do it. I wanted to understand this house, but opening drawers was a step too far. I would see something that caught my eye each visit to the house. I didn't want to find Mr. Willow still there but he always was.

When I was downstairs in the house it felt like he was above me, watching through the floor, up there on the ceiling like a spider looking down.

I picked up the bowl, and went out into the dark hallway, past the ticking ancestors in the clock and into the front room.

The room was dusty, though Maman and I had cleaned it when we first started looking after Mr. Willow. There were two easy chairs arranged around the fireplace with small nest of tables, stacked hunched under one another. A stage set for company. The cabinet over there in the far right corner had glass doors with a small key poking out of the front. The wood looked like shiny toffee. Glassy brown.

Inside it, cut crystal wine glasses, three or four vases, some glass plates, some white with patterns of ivy and a small china tea service.

This was the locked life of a woman, genteel and delicate and nothing of Mr. Willow. This room really didn't feel as if it was the room of a man living alone. The rag rug on the floor brought together the square between the chairs in one small rainbow, yet it gave out no brightness. Its thick pile had gathered dust and turned its landscape into an overcast day. It was a cloud ready to rain dust if it was hit. A sand storm of years of skin. The museum of this room was so quiet and still.

I heard groaning upstairs that broke the spell and I walked up the stairs, holding the bowl of stew. He turned towards me into the door frame as I had come to it. Like he was the door on the hinge. He was out of his bed again!

Mr. Willow turned his face to me. One eye, open.

Once, when I went to see the bird box in spring I walked over to it to see if a family had nested and made its home. As I put my face close to look in, peeping out of the little hole above the perch and below the upturned V of the roof of the house was a big black eye. It was such a shock to see that black eye. My head threw itself backwards, desperate to get away. It was a rat looking out of the box. It had got itself in there, probably sucking and crunching the nest of eggs it had found.

"What a shock you had," Maman had said at the time, laughing.

Maman had said I had called rats "battles" as a child. I think it was just a sound I liked or I'd heard it in the name at the time, but hearing it again, made so much sense. Rats spent heir whole lives not being seen, taking things, chewing their way through walls to food, through bins, stealing eggs, taking a life, to live. That eye.

His eye.

His ratty eye full of eager, looking at me now, it gave me the shivers. Back then I had run back into the cottage to tell Maman and Pops of the intruder. When they came out of course it had left the bird's house, along with all that new wonderful potential life and song inside the shells. Eaten away with shards of egg shells left.

Here it was again. Mr. Willow with the same eye gleaming, in the nest, cracked eggs open and spilling out.

He whispered, whether that was because of his weak chest or because I was close to him I didn't know. "Why doesn't the boy come to give me the soup?"

"I don't know what you mean, Mr. Willow," I said, moving forward past him to put his bowl of food down by the bed. "It's Maman and me that look after you."

I had got back out of the room past his swinging body and was stepping close the top of the stairs, feeling with my foot for the step.

"I think that's all for now Mr. Willow," I stammered. "Maman will be here later to light a fire and bring you something to eat."
I said it while turning, almost falling just to get away from him.

He laughed that squeaky dry laugh.

"The boy, the boy, the boy," he sang, like a little jig.

The turning arm of a music box, a short melody set to repeat from the start until the winding gave in. How long did he have left giving me clues? How long did I have before all this was gone? Sewing a seam to find things in this madness knowing the thread was getting shorter, I went dizzy, held myself against the wall. Cold stone. Taking the heat out of my leaning shoulder and giving me something to concentrate on.

I wondered if he would still be there, swinging like a door, when Maman came later, or like the rat in the bird box, one eye peeking out of the hole, he was waiting for his chance to run.

I wanted him gone. All my love for natural things, the beauty in animals, shells, plants, had gone in his company. He wasn't natural. He wasn't even a rat. He was alive but like fire.

I tiptoed upwards again and leaned back into the room, the frail man was still there singing in a thin reedy voice and unaware of me, or even the big sky behind the window.

He was moving his bony hands in the air, winter branches bobbing on trees, conducting himself and his stupid song.

"Tomorrow I will bring the soup," I said to him.
He turned but kept on singing with his moss teeth on show.

"I will bring the soup that Maman made for you, and I will tip it down the sink!" I said louder.
Dusk clouds were passing heavily over the blue sky behind him,

cruel and dark and outside like my words to Mr. Willow. Turning away from its door framed picture, I slammed that door behind me. I wanted to put out all the lights in the house and make dark all of the things he said to me that crawled like black insects under my skin.

"No more of your secrets in me. No more," I thought, scratching at my skin to get them off.

Chapter 33

Walking into the kitchen, there was the whole dinner service set of our family, sitting down at the table in their usual places. Maman starting to load the plates up with food. I went to the sink and even though I had washed the bowl at Mr. Willow's I felt the need to wash it again before putting it in the cupboard. I knew it was clean but the smell of his house was still in my nose. The ashes of his burning words rested and sunk on the pattern of the bowl, underneath the glaze. I scrubbed at my hands as well as the bowl. The nail brush was sharp from not being wet under the tap enough. Sloughing off the top layer of skin and making my hands red sore. I reached for the towel and turned back towards the table wiping and wiping hand to hand. The pain from washing and rubbing was helping me come back to my world instead of Mr. Willow's. The plates that Maman had served with food were put in front of everyone and I sat down to join everyone eating. Maman's cooking filled us all and for all the hours it took to make, the plates were empty in just a few minutes. I piled them up and took them to the sink and sat back down.

Frank was showing David and John his new watch. It seemed so big and bright. A full moon sitting on his wrist. Frank's wrist was too thin for it really and the strap was flopping long after the buckle.

"Bloke today wanted to put a bet on," he said. "I said I'd put it on for him if he gave me his watch, if he won he could have half winnings and his watch back."

"What happened?" asked David.

Everyone laughed including John. It was a gift of a moment, the brothers as a three again.

Frank and David included John in things much more now than when the accident first happened. No one knew how to be with him, back then, but now that everyone could understand him, well it made a big difference. What had split them apart, was filling in over time.

Out of all of them, John had changed the least. He rarely left the cove.

John and Pops were at the Smugglers. Of course they were.

He took each day as it came, each customer's glass taken back to the bar, one at a time with a methodical slowness as if he were conserving his energy for the length of his life doing the same job.

He fitted in well at the Smugglers, his presence didn't jar the regulars, everyone knew what had happened to him and there was a generosity towards him and his slow time taking. He was holding things just under the surface, letting them sleep, but sleeping things wake. When he would laugh at the pub, Pops said, it would be so loud people would move backwards away from the *ack ack* of his machine gun. When it came out his laughing was almost crying. The two were always so close together in John.

For all the times that he had been mean to me, for all his anger and frustration, I felt his love. I was his translator but no one needed me to understand him anymore, now I read his eyes more than his speech, reading what others can't.

Mr. Willow and his outbursts are small, like seeds, but I didn't swallow them. The shock of hearing them took my breath away and when I finally took a breath back I inhaled his secrets into my lungs. Now they sit in the warm wetness of my rib cage.

If your lungs are as dark and warm as soil, a seed will grow in there. It will sprout and unfold and double and double until it becomes hard to breathe. Your chest will hurt like you are drowning. Your lungs and your heart are squeezed. Breathing will ache from trying to get past the branches of the secret tree, as it grows.

I hate that I can't think, I hate that I can't breathe.

"What is stopping me from telling John?" I say to myself with gritted teeth.

Why should Mr. Willow have me, use me for his horrible secrets to live in? He's spat his black bile heart again and I need to wash it away. Why should John only have shadows of truth? That wasn't fair. Grabbing at things, not able to hold and turn the thing around in his hand. To have all the facts. I could help him catch the real story.

Once a truth is spoken and heard, it's already shifting shape in that person's ear. And then it's not yours to own the way you hear it anymore.

What if I don't tell it quite right?

What if I change the story in the retelling?

But enough.

Enough of this inside me world.

I am starting to sound like Bunny.

Soft Bunny who wants everyone to be good. Just like me before all this. When I don't like him, it's when he is me. *Stop.* Shine a light on Mr. Willow and cut John loose from his dark place.

That is how simple it has to be.

John was holding a mug with both hands, in the kitchen, in a daydream. His face was looking up and I wondered where he was in inside his head. If he was running fast like he used to.

I stood close and said to John.

"Will you help me with something upstairs?"

"What?" he said, shaken out of his daydream.

"Will you just help me?" I said.

His chair slid backwards on the quarry tiles and he stood up slightly annoyed.

"I dunno why it has to be me?" he said.

"Bad luck!" said Frank egging him on.

I walked up stairs. I felt him behind me, close, shuffling into the room. My mind started stirring all the information round, like Maman in front of a stew.

"What is it, Rozel? Me and the boys are playing cards tonight," John said. "Whatever it is you need help with, why you chose me over the others I don't know. Either of them are better at most things than me now."

He smiled as he said it, but it didn't last long. John still moved his arms about when he talked. His gesturing was how he got what he wanted to say out, back when no one understood him. It had stuck. I really loved it. I really loved this John.

"Sit," I said putting my hand on the bed.

He did a little curtsy to show me he thought I was being bossy.

It made me laugh. He smiled at me laughing, came and sat. I looked at him. His beautiful long face, his wonky lop sided expression from the fall and maybe a little from the two people that he held sewn together inside, acceptance and revolt.

I looked at the kinder side of his face and his silky floppy hair hanging down like curtains. He had grown his hair, to hide the scars from the stitches, it really suited him. He looked like the prince in my ladybird book who had put his crown down to dance.

"What," he said, impatient. "Come on!"

"Mr. Willow is nuts," I said.

"You brought me upstairs to tell me that?" he said, hitting the bed spread with his hand.

I could feel he was at the end of his rag. I didn't rise to it.

"No," I said calmly. "Mr. Willow was talking, not to me but he was talking out loud and I was there. He thought the grate in the room was a hole and he was talking to a boy. A boy called Stanley. He was talking like he'd made the hole to trap him and was throwing food down to him. Then he was asking about you? Asking why you didn't visit." I paused without looking up but to get a breath. "I think he made that hole for you and I think he's done it before." I bit my lip trying to get it all out the right way. "But he's also imagining people in his room, like they are actually there, so I don't know what he says is real or not! He's dying and on the way he's living in a different world."

"John?"

"John?"

I stopped. Looked up to see how all this had landed.

I didn't know if this was the right thing. Was I doing the right thing telling him? Now it was out of the box and I couldn't put it back in.

"John? John. Are you okay? I had to tell you, didn't I?"

John was sitting on the bed, looking at me. No, he wasn't looking at me he was looking past me. He was in that same world as Mr. Willow kept visiting, he was dreaming himself there, in front of me.

"John."

I was touching and rubbing his arm.

He blinked, looked down at his arm and then looked at me. This time he really was looking at me.

He smiled. Warm and vacant.

"John, are you okay? John! Where are you going?"

He didn't answer, he'd stood up and walked out. He didn't look back, walked down the stairs in a kind of trance.

Downstairs there was no talking just the sound of the kitchen door opening then closing.

"Rozel?" shouted Maman. "Where's John gone?"

I looked out the bedroom window and saw John heading for Mr. Willow's house.

"Oh, Hell," I said.

"OH, *HELL*," I yelled.

I ran down stairs and grabbed hold of Maman.

"He's going to kill Mr. Willow."

"What?" said Maman, looking bewildered. "What are you talking about?"

"It's what I said to him Maman!" I cried. "I told him what crazy things Mr. Willow had said on my visits. I told him he was talking to a boy in a hole. Like he'd dug the hole for him to fall into. He dug the hole for Stanley."

"What?" said Maman shaking her head and trying to piece what I was saying. "Stanley? Stanley was his brother. He died when they were young. All his siblings died. Poor man. Until it was just him."

Only me and Maman had been talking to each other, but the brothers and Pops had come towards us like a shoal of fish, swimming as one, we all moved together towards the door.

"John!" I shouted into the dark. "John. Stop!"

I was hoping the front door was locked at Mr. Willow's. I couldn't remember if I had put it on the latch or not.

My mind was checking the door, taking me there quicker than my body. I was imagining John entering the house and walking up the stairs past the clock. Stomping, getting bigger. John's teeth were growing longer, fur on his back, him as a wolf, Mr. Willow a thin rabbit. We all ran towards the house.

No sign of John. He must have moved fast.

The house was a way off still but I could see the door was open. A black, open square into the hallway. He hadn't even switched the hall lights on, I thought silently. John was in the house.

"Oh Hell," I said again in heaving breaths, trying to go faster. My legs gave, I fell to the ground. Frank pulled me up. Running across our common, I got second wind. I managed to keep going, my legs taking themselves forward, faster until I got ahead of the others, pulling nearer to John.

The rhythm of the jolt in my legs, up to my hips and the gulp of air into my beating heart.

Running.

Running.

Running.

Stop.

The door was open.

It was quiet.

The clock was ticking.

Floor.

Stairs.

Walls.

All leading me the way he had gone.

I took the stairs by twos, heaved myself up hard with my arms, pulling at the banister like thick rope to moor a boat.

I dived into the room, still leaping like I was on the stairs. John was there, stood over the bed. He turned to me. Tears in his eyes. Mr. Willow was in bed.

Dead.

Chapter 34

John turned to me, tears still streaming down his face.

"What have you done, John?" I said.

"He was dead when I got here," he said.

I looked at Mr. Willow. His face was not the peaceful look you assume with a dead person. He looked afraid. Afraid of where he was going, I thought.

I could hear the others scrambling into the room.

"Oh God, oh God," said Maman. She was breathing so heavy. Like she was drowning in the air, a fish. Huge big heaves of breath that were moving her whole body up and down in and out to get more air in. A jelly fish fighting against the tide.

"He was dead when we got here," I said. "I came in the same time as John, we saw him like this together."

John squeezed my hand. The blood rushed into it. I felt his thanks. Whatever reason I did it, it was my secret this time.

I was okay with that.

I was at John's side and that was how it was. How it should be. My John.

"Look at him. The bastard," said John and spat in his face.

The spit hit Mr. Willow's dead face just below his eye. It ran down his grey cheek like a tear.

A crying, stone statue bringing people to pray at their feet.

"John!" said Maman and leaned forward rubbed the spit off his face with her apron. She pushed John in the stomach, backwards away from the bed, roughly.

"He did it Maman," said John. "He kept me in that hole!"

His voice sounded like John as a child, telling on one of us to Maman.

"It was him that kept me there," he was leaning on the wall to steady himself. "I knew it; I knew it but I couldn't know it. Oh, God! I can remember his face, Maman. Looking down on me. Maman!" He cried. "It was him! All this time! Him. He did this to me."

He was shaking, not able to keep his lop-sided body against the wall, his profile cut out wrong where the scissors slipped.

"He's gone now. He's escaped. But what about me? I wanted to tell him that I knew now. I wanted him to say to me, to admit it was him, but he's gone! It's not fair, but, but I'm glad he's dead!" he said and sort of fell further back, the solid wall seeming to falter to catch him. I reached for him. He slid down the wall until he was on the floor. A rag doll, legs splayed. His energy had completely gone from him.

Pops, for all his small frame, grabbed him and held him tight. John was so much bigger that Pops, but it was like he was a little child being held up by him. Like the photo of him learning to walk, his arms out stretched. Pops had got him. He held him there in that scrunched up half sitting half standing shape. Being the strong legs John needed.

John was convulsing, big shakes. For a moment I thought he was having a fit, his body jerking violently into Pops. Pops had held him many times in a fit, with his hands bruised behind his head to protect John hitting it on a hard floor. But this wasn't a fit, it was a year of tears.

Frank and David were stood in the doorway, whispering, "Hell!" and looking at each other, then back to Mr. Willow, the face of Frank's new watch matching their white faces. Holding onto the door frame each side, filling the space.

Mr. Willow let out a high sigh.

"Oh God love us!" yelled Maman, who was closest to the bed. She had put her hands up to her head, in defence.

We all stopped and looked at him. There was no sign of breathing. All I could hear was a heavy pounding of my blood hitting my ears drum.

Was he alive?

He still looked dead. But then he had looked dead most of the year.

Maman grabbed his hand, felt at his wrist. Her two fat fingers pressing at the slack skin covered wrist bone.

"There is a pulse!" said Maman, looking at Pops in shock. "He's still alive! Should I call the doctor? What should I do? Pops, what should we do?"

All Maman's questions were aimed over our heads past us, at Pops.

Pops stood John up. He brushed John down as if he had fallen in the dirt, straightening his clothes He looked at John, close to his face, ruffled his hair and cupped the back of his head in a strong tender way.

His voice was deep and strong. "Frank, David, take John back to the house. Rozel, Maman get out with the brothers and go back too, I will deal with this."

No one questioned Pops.

We stood up and walked out of the room, leaving Pops in there with Mr. Willow.

The walk back to the cottage was silent. Ahead of Maman were the three brothers. John was in the middle with an arm on either shoulder of Frank and David. They were revellers coming home from the pub. John's legs, soft and bendy and making the motion of walking but mainly being dragged by the brothers.

Maman had her hand in mine. She was holding on with interlocking fingers, her arm outstretched backwards as she ploughed forward ahead of me. The grip was too tight and it was making my eyes water. I said nothing. Each of the bones on my fingers pushing the blood into my purple fingertips. I knew it was her love holding me tight. And the pain felt good in a way, it meant I wasn't dead.

Back at the cottage, the brothers had sat John in between them at the table and David had his arm over him to stop the shaking. John was still crying. Would he ever be able to stop now he had started, opened the gates? Maman went straight over to the sink, reached underneath and pulled out the Christmas brandy. She told David to get some glasses. She put a fingers width of it in everybody's glass, leaving one for Pops. I sat sipping at the table. The liquid burned. First my tongue then a long line down my throat and as I breathed in, the air felt cold going into me. All three brothers necked down in one fast motion. No one wanted to break the spell with words. No one knew which words to use.

The brandy was still burning me as my small sips went down. I felt my tongue go numb while tasting old cherries.

I looked at John's eyes, a clear sky after rain. He looked back at me. I looked at Frank, his eyes like a copper coin, brown with warm metal running through like wire. David looked up at me from the table, his sad brown eyes, deep dark pools of a faithful dog. They were such a dark brown they melted into the pupil. Maman did not look up. She was glancing at Frank's watch then at Pops' full glass. Her hands were worrying themselves like they did when her mind was running, trying to find busy.

John's shoulders were shaking as more huge tears came down his cheek, rolling down like the spit on Mr. Willow's grey face when he had spat at him.

Maman stood up, filled his glass with more brandy then she bent down, while standing behind him and hooked her arms round his chest and up towards his neck. She rested her forehead on top of his head and whispered.

"It's alright, my love, it will be alright."

About an hour later, I couldn't be sure because time goes faster and slower in strange times, Pops arrived back at the kitchen.

Maman looked at him.

He looked at Maman.

I think they had spoken to each other in that look.

He came over to us, to the table. Took his glass, necked the whole thing that had taken me an hour to sip. Slammed it down on the table. Bang. He looked at John, not at Maman this time.

"That's that," he said.

Chapter 35

Between the triplets and me, there had been a baby.

Maman never spoke of it.

It was her darkness, the thing she buried that would never green spear up and turn to flowers.

When the bleeding came no one knew what to do because the triplets were little and who would stay with them and who would take Maman?

So Maman lay in bed with all three boys bleeding and crying while Pops went out into the night in a huge panic to get the doctor. When he got back, Maman had the baby out of her. The cord was still inside her and the baby had the other end. Tied together.

Maman had tried to breathe life into the wet creature. She had blood round her mouth from kissing its face.

Two of the boys were crying. But their noise, although loud was not making any impact on the scene Pops came back to.

The doctor and Pops were at a loss of where to begin to untie all of it. They started by getting the triplets into their own cot. Maman would have to be separated from the dead baby. But it just seemed an impossible task, in that moment with her looking down at what she had found and lost all in one go.

Days later with Maman still in bed, she had all her sisters around her, sorting the washing, playing with the boys.

Pops was digging a hole in the garden. He had spent all his time building a box and trying to get the image of Maman surrounded by babies and blood round her mouth out of his mind. Maman was obviously doing the same from the other side of the glass.

Either side of a window separated by the grief, though Pops barely knew the baby, Maman had carried it inside, felt it kick, felt it move.

As the weeks and months passed after the baby had gone, Pops was pushed backwards and away from the cottage by the strong current of Maman's rolling grief. She raged over why it had happened to them. What had they done to deserve it? Maman hurried herself about not giving herself time to sit or think. Those were the times that brought the sadness back.

I'm not proud of how I know all this. Maman got a lot of her letters to Sylvie back. I found them and took the top one to read.

She said to Sylvie that Pops knew he was hers but she needed more space around her for the pain.

That's when he found a place that was his at the far end of the bar in the Smugglers. He could sit there and pass nothing but the time, measured by a slowly drunk pint. It was his spot, second stool from the end and he felt moored there. His harbour calmer than the sea beyond the walls, the shore within his walking depths.

Chapter 36

Maman was on her hands and knees.

She was digging at the earth. She didn't have her trowel or the spade or her basket. I thought we had had the last of the potatoes. She'd made a leek and potato soup last week saying, "That's the last of them, Pops!"

I had stirred the pan for her, watching the circular coins of leeks soften and string out into seaweed. She had thrown in the chicken stock she had boiled from the bones and the sweet steam pushed cracks into the skim of fat on the top.

This wasn't where the potatoes were planted.

She had her back to the cottage and this kitchen window I was looking from. She was in her blue apron, I could see the ties around her back and the neck loop catching stray hairs at her neck. She knelt forwards, with her backside in the air, then rest it down, sitting on her feet and covering them with her dress either side.

She kept hitting her head on the rose bush where she was digging, the thorn bush jiggled. She rubbed at her face, presumably to wipe away the scratches from the thorns. Pops was out of the cove, helping someone in the next parish fix their tractor.

"The gear stick had got stuck then just slipped down into the mechanics of it," Pops said over dinner.

I said, "Was it like a black and white film, I think it was Fred Astaire in a top hat tap dancing with a cane. In the dance he taps a table then lifts the cane up in the air holds the base of it and lets it slide down through his hand to the floor and then carries on dancing. Was it like that?"

"No," said Pops, gently smiling putting his hand onto mine.

John was upstairs in the bath and I didn't know where the other brothers were. I was the only one downstairs.

I was washing the breakfast bowls, scrubbing at the harder bits of porridge that had dried on. Maman wasn't aware of me on the other side of the kitchen window. It felt a bit like being in her room when she wasn't there. She had dug a fair way down, then she stopped, hands down, still. She lifted a box onto the piled earth. I couldn't see what it was. I just kept on scrubbing in the warm water, looking out at her, and down to see if I'd unstuck the porridge. She was lifting the box.

Her body was heaving up and down in her blue dress, a stormy sea and she was wiping at her face with the cleaner backs of her hands.

I stood on my tiptoes, pushed myself higher on the sink trying to see into the box from here.

I thought I could see something. No. Just me in the glass.

Her hand was inside the box, stroking it. She was rocking hard now, forward so far, I thought she would fall into that hole. All the holes our family keep falling into.

John's hole, if you can call it that, was filled in by the parish after he was found in it, so it doesn't even count now.

Maman turned to the cottage. She had been wiping her face and the soil on her hands had dirtied her face. I could see her tears had made a watery path, through the dirt and down her face like the stream down the cliff that runs into the sea.

I put my soapy hands up and waved.

I couldn't see if she could see me in the window. The light was hitting it and it seemed as if she looked at me, but she was looking straight through me, back at the reflection of herself.

She turned back to the scene, closed the lid of the box, put it in the hole and started pushing soil from each side back into the hole.

A few minutes later she was back inside and going straight upstairs to wash her hands.

She had told John to get out of the bath and stood on the landing. He had said something to her, muffled from behind the door and I had run to the bottom of the stairs and shouted, "He said he's almost finished," even though I didn't need to translate.

"Thank you," said Maman, in a voice that felt like it was caught at the back of her throat. I heard the lock click and Maman and John slid past each other on the top landing without a word. Johns face seemed puffy when he came down and I suspected he used the bath as a place to cry. Maman closed the doors behind her and had been in the room for a while longer than it took to wash her hands. I really needed the toilet but didn't want to rush Maman so I went outside to see if I could see the blackbird's nest. I looked around hopping on one leg then the other, then went back in. I heard the door unlock upstairs and Maman came down the stairs, lifting her apron off. The edges of her hair were pulled back and wet she had splashed water on her face that was as puffy as John's.

Chapter 37

Everyone from the cove was there outside the church, which wasn't exactly a crowd.

It had taken two weeks for the funeral to be arranged, mainly because he had no next of kin. Well, that wasn't entirely true. There was a nephew on the mainland, but he had refused to do anything after hearing that Mr. Willow had given everything he owned to Mrs. Bertram.

Mrs. Bertram had no idea why Mr. Willow had put her in the Will.

"That's what she's saying to anyone that dares ask her!" Maman said to Pops. "But mostly she tries to just change the subject."

Everybody in the cove was gossiping and coming up with different ideas for why he'd done it.

It was just like him, to start the whispering and mistrust after he was gone.

I was glad that Mrs. Bertram and Bunny knew nothing of what had happened that night at Mr. Willow's house. No one asked Pops what happened after we'd left. I couldn't think for too long about Pops there. Maybe he sat with him til his last breath. Maybe he didn't.

I hated the idea that Pops might get some of Mr. Willow's black bile.

Whatever Pops did that night, he made sure that the rest of the family had no involvement in it. We didn't see, hear or know how Mr. Willow left this world. As far as we were concerned he'd died once that night. It was only Maman who had felt his pulse. Maybe she had lied, just as I had lied about getting there the same time as John? Had John tried to kill him before I had got there, or was he dead already?

The answer to most of my questions ended with Pops, and he said even less than usual.

A weight had lifted off John. He knew for certain what had happened, that it had been a deliberate act. It wasn't his fault and that made all the difference. He began to laugh mistakes off, laugh more generally. John was back.

Mr. Willow had used the best disguise of all, taking it to his grave. He had remained his weird and creepy self to the end, too obvious a suspect to be involved.

"When people show you again and again who they are you should really believe them," Maman said shaking her head at all we had missed.

We shuffled forward through the arched wooden doors.

The church echoed with our feet and the sound of the bright organ in the cold air. The front row was just our family, Mrs. Bertram and Bunny. No one sat in the next few pews, out of respect or reserving them for people closer to him, but they remained empty for the whole service.

Further back, a few other people from the cove, the Smugglers Inn lot mainly, the doctor and his wife and then the odd older person who we weren't sure who they were. Had they known him when they were younger? Maman said she saw old friends mainly at funerals now.

"They become the new parties as you get older," she whispered with a short laugh.

Mr. Willow was not family or friend to any of us sitting there.

He was gone and what was left, just a body in a box.

I felt claustrophobic looking at the coffin, like I was inside it instead of Mr. Willow. Church made me feel closed in. The Vicar told everyone when they had to sit, stand and sing and the rest of the time be as quiet as possible. I wanted to jump up or scream, with the stiffness of it all, though I never would. His coffin was walnut wood, swirling patterns with a high sheen like the toffee wood cabinet in his front room. It was an open casket resting high on a table, shorter than the tall cupboards in his house but I had no intention of snooping into this one. I saw the silky white interior, pleated and cushioned, bulking out the inside edge. I kept my eyes down and my head low enough so as not see anything til the lid went on. He had haunted me long enough being alive those past months and I still thought of the dead horse.

Besides, we'd seen him rise from the dead once before and the sooner that lid went on the better. There was no baby needing his skin coat cutting off to put on another man, as sure as the sky was the sky, we weren't going to dig him up after he'd gone in the ground.

We listened to the simple sermon, plain and without heart or feeling. No one took a reading. We sang *Jerusalem*. And then it was over. The front row, all of us crying for what had been taken from John. This was a place where we could cry together for John without anyone knowing. We were hiding in plain view. We were crying for everyone but Mr. Willow. The rest of the church would have seen our tears as grief for his body in the box.

He was being buried now. Out of sight.

It was our turn to watch him get lowered into a hole. John had kept back from the edge. Pops had a tight grip on Maman's hand and mine. Frank nudged David, with his elbow, as if he was going to push him in. Mrs. Bertram didn't look like herself. She was too neat. Bunny was distant, his mind elsewhere, but then everything and everyone had an odd echo today.

He said something to his mother that made her stop walking, then he strode away, ahead of us all and I couldn't catch up with him. He'd reached the wall of the graveyard and I didn't think it was right to shout after him at a funeral, even Mr. Willow's.

Ever since talking about John on top of the tower, we had drifted. He hadn't been strong for me, against Mr. Willow. I had got so tied up with John, that I hadn't visited the cliff or the tower, so he knew nothing of what we had done on the dying night, and I hadn't made the time to tell him.

Pops was talking quietly to Mrs. Bertram in the graveyard. She nodded then shook her head then nodded again. Maman, oblivious to their intense chat and was talking to the vicar, who in his slow way was talking about flowers and gardens and his favourite vegetables to grow.

Maman truly loved talking about gardens. She cooed at the idea of being given different lettuces to grow and revelled at his idea of tomatoes growing in a hanging basket. It was a summer fête, them both chatting of things growing right beside a newly planted Mr. Willow.

John clapped his hands in the air for attention and said, "Everyone, we'll meet in the Smugglers."

And off he went, and the small crowd followed him like a leader.

I stood on my own near Maman and the Vicar, who were rounding off their conversation, near enough to hear them but I could only see Pop's conversation. Stood on the Willow's family plot, even more land they own, one big head stone, lonely as Mr. Willow. On it was a long list of names followed by plain flat stone for the names to come as time took them.

Richard.

Bunny.

Stanley.

Arthur.

So he'd had four brothers. Richard had died in childbirth, cause the dates were the same, the other three died before I was born.

Loving Mother.

Loving Father.

Loving Son.

The words were worn shallow in the stone and the dates not easily read.

Carving dates into stone is hammering through time. The words last as the stone is taken out to make the letters. What happens to the stone that gets taken out for the carving? I'm standing on the tiny stones on the path wondering if these are names? I'm reading who's buried here from stone that isn't there. My name will be the path one day.

Maman's soft fleshy arm linked into mine and I turned to her. Her body was always warm. Here she was again, pushing away my sea fret thoughts.

"Come on sweet girl, let's drink one down, eh?" she spoke in a song.

Her pansy made up face, turned to me as if I were the sun, delicate and open as ever and always.

My Loving Mother I carved into the air above us.

Chapter 38

My body switched on and I sat up. I could hear the clock tick its footsteps in the snow towards me. An even tick, working its way through time. It won't be rushed. I lie back and the ticks get louder for the listening. I had put it at the bottom of the stairs, just like it had been at Mr. Willow's house. I guessed that it wouldn't be in the sunlight and it could be heard upstairs and downstairs. It was all new to me, owning something so I took the advice of where it had been before it was mine.

After Mr. Willow died, I got a letter from his solicitors with a notice that I had been given the clock. First it had gone to Mrs. Bertram along with the rest of his will. She was the main benefactor. But they had found amongst his things an un-posted hand written letter.

It had said, "Rozel took on my bad health and well-being. She reminds me of the horse. The soup was good. Give her the clock for the stories we shared."

They gave me the letter to read. It must have been written in the last weeks of his life. The shaky writing in black ink had mistakes crossed out and drops of ink splattered here and there where the pen had stuck and jabbed and sprayed. The signature at the bottom S. Willow in a huge flamboyant curving end looked ridiculous.

I stared at that paper for a long time. Holding it in my hands. It had only taken a moment to read through, I think the solicitors thought I was re-reading the letter to understand why he would give me a gift. I was looking next to his signature, the speck of spilt black ink, a round black dot. A hole.

Maman wasn't mentioned in the letter. Not once. She was used to her jobs being unseen, it didn't even enter her mind that she had been treated unfairly. She was the cleaner, the invisible staff. In all of her jobs at "the big houses" on the cliff, I doubt if any of the families knew her first name.

She did the work that didn't happen. As far as that world of big houses was concerned, she wasn't there.

It was strange to even think like that because in our family she was the monument, the huge pin holding the cottage's walls together. The least invisible thing in our lives. If anyone in our family was invisible it was David or Pops, pushing themselves back into a crowd. Learning by listening, looking out.

All the family were struck by the news, the clock was the grandest thing in our cottage. It was a guest. Frank had immediately wanted to find out how much the clock was worth.

That's how Frank saw the whole world. Everything was about the money. Even money was about the money. It gave him a narrow view of everything including the cottage and the common. It was all about guessing what things would be worth, what would be the things to sell and what would be the things to save. He called it "just business". It felt like madness. It gave him an agitated unease with his lot. An itch that he scratched til it bled.

"What's it worth though? What's it worth?" he'd ask me over and over.

I said he could find out, just to shut him up, but not to tell me. I would have to take better care of it if it was worth a big pile of money and it would have a bigger voice in the cottage. I liked that it could be worth nothing except the years owned.

How much was a year worth?

I woke up to a Sunday of white New Year sun, streaming past the bare trees all the way into my room, a dreamy sadness. I had fallen asleep last night with the curtains open, watching the wind pulling at the scene outside. Now the seagulls were bouncing and lifting on the invisible air while, inside the cottage, the clock ticked a sad step that couldn't get itself up the stairs, or outside in the air.

The clock inside.

The seagulls outside.

Counting the bird calls and the ticks. A song started to play in my head. *I'm making each moment count.* It was such a fleeting tune, there then gone, that it could have been a car going past with its radio on. Jangly and joyous. The way the song fell, a bell ding-donging, ringing out, The everything and nothing of this moment, the ghost of the song, only ever played in my head. Here I am between two worlds, just like Mr. Willow.

Chapter 39

Earlier that week, I had sat on a flat elephant grey rock listening to Bunny talking to me, out at a view, as he always did.

"Under the long fur of an otter there is another layer of fur, short and so dense that you can't see the skin underneath. This is so they don't freeze to death when they are out fishing." Bunny was pointing at the otter rolling itself on a rock covered with seaweed.

"They are so like dogs, rolling on stinking stuff," I said in reply.

This was us, talking out to sea.

The seaweed smell put most tourists off our bay and the next harbour to us. It came in thick black strips and as it dried it popped, the smell clung to the air and wouldn't let go.

I found it sweet and silky, a smell I had known forever.

I closed my eyes and traced myself back through all my visits to this cove, to this beach at this time of the day. The different sizes of me sniffing the green air. Time slows down into still rock pools. Bunny kept looking down at his watch. He was meeting friends later down at the harbour. Him checking the time was taking our moment of time away from us.

The watch on his arm, my clock at the bottom of the stairs. Both facing us. A reminder of Mr. Willow. He'd said, "What if he was my dad?" out towards the horizon. The thing Bunny had said started to slide under the water and disappear like the otters. There was no air to keep the words up here at the surface. I didn't have an answer and neither did Bunny and those sorts of thoughts are just too heavy to float.

I couldn't see him in the ink scrawl or the wiry body of Mr. Willow. Sometimes I couldn't see him as belonging to anyone but me. We watched as the otters resurfaced, played around and then swam round the bigger rocks.

Otters hold hands at night so they don't get lost or float away from each other. Maman told me that one night as she stroked my head when I couldn't sleep. Maman, my otter.

I stood up off the rock and felt how much heat the rock had taken from me as I'd sat, stiff and cold legs like wood clambered me back towards the sand.

The following morning, Bunny went out on the main fishing boat with Frank, David, and Seth, whose dad owned the boat. I had heard them before seeing them in the kitchen, when the light was still grey and thick in my room. Scuffling about, chairs scrapping and stifled laughter downstairs, shushing each other. I had stayed and listened, flat on my back on the bed, me, the ceiling above their heads eavesdropping.

Their trip had been planned for ages, each time remembering another thing to do or bring, lines, hooks, nets. The giddy excited voices rolling up in volume then bringing it back down. As the brothers grew older, there was less running and shouting in the cottage. They would come and sit at the kitchen table, walk up the stairs. Doors got closed not slammed. The tick of the clock could be heard above everyone.

It was nice to hear this joy moving around. The back door shut and I heard the voices move to my window now instead of the floor, sloping off outside, letting their voices rise higher now without the ceiling.

I got up and moved to the window to look at them. Dark figures with bouncing strides, hitting each other on shoulders, outlines of puppets, strung up and dancing. The jerky jolliness was infectious and I laughed a small breath onto the cold pane that misted them out of view. But oh my, the morning air was cold and I jumped back into my bed covers, shivering, visions of the cold sea splash and wet ropes being undone on the boat. I snuggled back down, warming the sheets, then the sheets warming me, then turned over and slipped back into a warm sea sleep.

I woke up from a bad dream. I was hot and the covers looked like I had fought with them. Still the dreams I dream come to get me, my night enemies.

With Bunny gone for the day, I thought I would go and see Mrs. Bertram up on the cliff.

There was so much gossip about her getting everything in the will from Mr. Willow. It was all people seemed to talk about.

Was she secretly part of his family? Mrs. Bertram had always been a talking point, well before this. In that way that women choose to talk quietly about women who sit outside of their circle.

Maman says, "When a new thing happens or a new person comes here, most people shrug them off. It's easier than understanding."
I think Maman wanted me to understand. She went on: "Traditions and ways of doing things keep history happy. Then they don't have to learn a new thing, they can use the old ways and go back to sleepwalking in what they know."

Mrs. Bertram had lived on the cliff as long as I had known her and Bunny. She lived on the edge of people too. If someone doesn't engage in a small place, people naturally think they are too good for them. Maybe because her house did look down on everything in the cove that's why they felt she did too. Of course they were never impolite in the queue at the post office or at the shop or when she passed on the bike. I always heard a hello and a how are you, and I wasn't always sure how much of the side talk Mrs. Bertram knew was being directed her way. A single mother who lived with her son on a cliff was enough for most of the women to judge. After she was out of ear-shot, they would pull together, itching to talk. Clucking chickens scratching at clues. "Did you know..." it would begin.

Was I so different to them? Wanting to know.

She lived the way she wanted and dressed for walking, climbing and running. Growing into a woman wasn't about becoming a statue like the other women.

When I was asked what I wanted to be when I was older, I wanted to say free or fox, but my answer was formed from the question. The answer they wanted was a job that had a name. I would say nurse.

I imagined myself nursing things like stars, and foxes and plants and rocks. A whole hospital of stars that were damaged from shooting across the sky, foxes that with their colour washed out from sleeping in the sun.

If someone asked me right now what I wanted to be when I

grew up, I would say Mrs. Bertram. She was the only adult I saw freewheeling down a hill with her legs out at either side. She'd surprise me, being on top of a roof with the silver fish gut on her face, or wearing her work overalls and her hair scraped back to not get in the way.

If I had to choose between being one of the women in the village watching Mrs. Bertram, or Mrs. Bertram doing things without a care, I would choose her every time.

Maman was a bridge between the two worlds of these women. She had an easy time at the shop and the post office. Maman's earthy pleasant way made people feel relaxed. She would hear the gossip that went on but not comment on it. She had learnt that from Pops I guess. This made her belong to it without adding what was said. Maman was slightly more cautious with Mrs. Bertram. I could tell in the way she stood when she was talking to her, the ground wasn't firm. They spent more time in each other's company because of Bunny and me.

Maman rarely spoke of the gossip.

If only I could hear what she thought. But here we are in our own worlds, our own heads.

If I started walking up the hill, it would sort out my rushing thoughts, I could plant them into the ground as I went. Walking sorts my head, especially the cliff path. You have to concentrate making the right step to not slip. There's the pushing of my hands down onto my thighs, to help my legs up the steepest parts, slapping a beat. The wind is coming off the sea, flying around the corner of the cliff in gusts. It pushes the air out of my mouth before it gets to my lungs. All of it calming my brain into quiet.

The noise of the world.

In the distance near the clean line of the horizon, I could see a boat. A dark, small thumb smudge. I wonder if that's the boys on their fishing trip? An insignificant dot, at the edge of my world. Small as an ant.

Down at the harbour wall there is a stone. On it is the name of all the fishermen who were lost at sea in a storm.

Eight names on top of each other in a list with "We Will Never Forget" arching above.

The carving is protected from the worst weather, facing half away from the sea, the carved words have softened with the sea spray and the air. The sea was ashamed of what it had done and wanted to rub those names out.

I would trace the letters with my fingers.

The most eroded letters were the 'o's and the 's's.

The curves had made wider holes. Almost the width of my finger and tracing these letters felt the best. A perfect road for my finger.

Each time, a dark mark near the bottom of the stone where a dog had come and cocked its leg to wee. I wonder if it was the same dog each time or all the dogs choose it.

I can't imagine an owner letting a dog wee on the memorial. To a dog it was just a stone. Really that is all it was, if you couldn't read.

We make objects hold more than their material. We give them names, we give them our lives.

My mind had walked itself all the way up the cliff and I was nearly at the end of the path going up.

The flat bit of path that came to the house was the most heart stopping because it had become a bridge with the land fallen away either side of it. If the rest of the path fell then the cottage would stand on its own bit of cliff, separate from the rest of the cove.

The wind comes upwards, each side of me here and my hair lifts up off my shoulder either side in a dance. I push it off my face as it hits my eyes.

Blinking over at the house, past my hair, its curtains closed. Where else would she be?

As I got to her door I could hear voices inside.

"Why do you think he gave you everything, Jessie?"

"I don't know!"

"Can you think of a reason? Can you make up a reason?"

I knew both voices.

I had not known 'til that point that Mrs. Bertram was called Jessie. Bunny had always called her mum, and everyone else including me,

Mrs. Bertram. So it felt strange to hear her first name. Jessie.

Stranger still it was Pops' voice that had said her name. He had said it easily, like he had said it many times before this point. I paused. I didn't know whether to knock or leave.

"I think you should go," I heard from inside.

The door opened. There they both were, looking at me in the doorway.

"How long have you been here, Rozel?" asked Mrs. Bertram.

"I — I just arrived. If you are busy?" I said, looking at Pops.

He had a look on his face that I hadn't seen before. I couldn't work it out.

"Pops was just leaving," said Mrs. Bertram. "Do you want to come in?"

"Okay," I said.

I walked in and saw two cups on the table, one chair was pushed back away. The kettle was on the stove, flowers resting on their side by the sink.

I thought about the 's's in the name Jessie wearing out quicker than the other letters on stone.

Is it only stone that wears out?

This is just a room.

Pops put his hand on my shoulder and walked out of the door that I had just walked into. He waved his hand in the air behind him as he went not looking back but seeming quite relaxed. I watched him go and saw Mrs. Bertram do the same, biting her lip. She shut the door, pushing back the wind from the sea cliff and locking it out. With the door shut, I felt quiet shelter after being so blown about. I sat down.

"So, Rozel, everything okay? You know Bunny is on his fishing trip." Mrs. Bertram was busying herself at the sink. She put the flowers flat into the sink square. Not upright, to drink water and to arrange, but flat and out of sight.

"What was Pops doing here?" I asked.

"Oh, I had a problem with the chimney again, there was smoke coming down when I first lit the fire. But it wasn't a fish this time." She laughed. "It was a bird's nest that had fallen in and got stuck. It's out now."

I looked at the fire, there was no mess around the hearth.

Pops came and fixed stuff for Mrs. Bertram, there were still things she needed fixing by him for all that she could do on her own.

"So when I arrived Pops was asking you about the Will, Mr. Willow's Will. Is that right?" I rubbed my finger on the smooth wood struts under the table.

Mrs. Bertram laughed. "I have never had so many people ask the same question in so many different ways. Not all of them with words. Most of them just look at me and I know it's the question they are asking to everybody but me."

She rolled her eyes up and her gaze stayed on a spider's web line wafting in the corner from a draught.

"Rozel, if I knew why that mad old man did that, I would sleep a whole lot better at night," she said.

I looked at her.

I hadn't really looked at her face this way before, as if it was new. It was weather worn, leather worn. Every time she opened her door, she'd be hit with salty sea air and that had beaten at her face into a smooth stone like a pebble from a rock. Today her hair was scraped back into a low ponytail then doubled round into a loop. There was halo made from hair that had come loose around the edges, a wispy golden float against the brown that was scraped back. It was a lion's mane made from thin silk cotton thread.

Her eyes: Bunny's, with a stainless steel sadness.

She sat down and looked up at me, I moved my gaze away from being caught by hers so I didn't lose my nerve.

"Mrs. Bertram, Mr. Willow said strange things to me when I was taking care of him," I said.

"Like what, Rozel?" She looked just like Pops had done at the door. Startled.

"He talked about a boy called Stanley."

"Stanley?" said Mrs. Bertram. "Stanley? I don't understand?"

She said it to herself, but out loud.

She came to the table and sat down. She looked at me. "Do you know who Stanley is?" she said to me.

"No," I said. "I thought he was talking about John, because it was like he was talking at someone in a hole."

She didn't seem to be fazed by any of it.

"Who was Stanley?" I said.

"You think Mr. Willow knew John was in the hole?" she said ignoring my question.

"Yes," I said. "And even though he was losing his mind, the things he saw when I was there, it was haunting him, what he'd done. Well, it felt that way watching it..." I tailed off.

Mrs. Bertram looked at me. I couldn't understand where she was in all this without words. Because she was alone a lot of the time, she didn't feel the need to smile or show expressions from thought, it carried over in company. Her face was blank. She could do really well with Frank and his poker.

She was picking at a loose thread on her cuff. Unlike Maman, her hands were nimble and long and she had wound it around her finger and once round, held tight, pulled and it was off. She let go of her grasp and the thread spiralled down to the floor, light and curling resting into an O on the stone.

She rubbed it with her foot and the O rolled together into a single plaited line.

"Who have you talked to about all of this?" She said, looking at me with no sign of where we were at. Scuffing her foot again, she looked down at the table, paused then up and said, "We weren't related."

Did she mean Stanley, Mr. Willow, or Pops?

She carried on scuffing her foot forward and back on the floor but the thread had gone, worn away or fallen down a crack. She looked coy and much younger than I had seen her look before, swinging her leg under the table.

"Do you mean Stanley?" I asked.

"No."

And then she just stood, walked up stairs, into her room and shut the door.

I was left there, at the table, wondering, should I wait for her? I stood up then sat down a few times trying to decide what to do. I must have looked ridiculous sitting and standing over again in the kitchen alone! At last sanity got the better of me and I left the cottage. I pulled at the door hard, with both hands to close as the wind kept on catching it, playing tug of war. And when I finally did manage to close it, it slammed hard. I wondered if Mrs. Bertram thought I had left in anger.

I didn't see her up at the window but I heard the clock chime its half hour once more. Stepping back into the wind and the sound of the waves, the chaos of inside and out, I wish I'd chosen to sit back down in the kitchen. Even though it was a couple of steps back through the door, that kitchen felt a long stretch away now. I left, headed down the path, whipping my legs with the course grass, it stung more than usual, I pulled my socks higher, but the scratching still came through, there was nothing to do but just let it happen and take it.

Pops was walking towards the Smugglers Inn. He saw me, lifted his arm up high in acknowledgement and carried on. He seemed to be walking quicker than before he'd seen me.

He reminds me of the crabs in the rock pools. If you lift a piece of seaweed or a rock, they would rush to the next hiding place. I hadn't known Pops was hiding until he scurried like a crab.

What happened up at the cottage tonight was something and nothing. There was nothing really to tell, nothing had actually happened had it? But there was enough to feel that I should keep it from Maman. Pops had visited Mrs. Bertram — Jessie — and by the close way they talked, done so often.

It made me feel disloyal to Maman. There was nothing I actually knew to tell her, but it made me shift around thinking about it. Maman was oblivious of these undercurrents and my guilty withhold. I would see Pops glance over at me at the mention of her or the house or Mr. Willow.

The thing between me and Maman was one sided, only I knew.But between me and Pops there was a two way knowing of it, going back and forth.

I wish I could ask him to tell me what it was I knew. Pops seemed unnerved by me, or by something. The two people I had always just assumed were the same as me, lived the same, a pair, had secrets from each other.

My memories are intact in a pure and perfect replica, at least I think that. In someone else, those very same memories have been painting the same room, in a different colour.

Maman carried on as if nothing happened, and of course that was the case for her.

I was looking for signs and signals to see if she sensed a change in me or Pops.

I did the same with Pops. I sat looking at how he talked to Maman.

His nightly trips to the Smugglers Inn, that had been a punctuation, unquestioned all my life, that he went there and nowhere else, I now questioned. I could have asked John simple questions about the Smugglers evenings, and Pops' movements, but I couldn't bring myself to have him unwittingly as my spy.

John and I had become closer still, since Mr. Willow had died. His outbursts had almost disappeared, he'd smile more often, putting his arm around me in an easy gesture. Maybe I had become a brother to him. I belonged again and so did he. We were all tied together from that night.

But what was Pops doing, for the good of all of us, with Mrs. Bertram?

Even before Bunny and me, when we were just friends I had wanted Mrs. Bertram to like me. Bunny called her Mrs. Bertram when I was around. Who was she beyond those words attached to her?

When I discovered our teacher's first name, Janet, hearing it and working out from their initial J, who they meant, it transformed her. She emerged transformed, into an alternative life, where people called out to her in a very different way, with love.

How names wrap around us, change the ways of being seen.

I had written her into my world as Bunny's mum. I believed every word she'd say as the truth, that same way I believed Maman and Pops.

Just then, it hit me that I took everybody at their word.

I'd found the truth hiding in Mr. Willow's wreck of a mind. I wasn't so stupid to believe that no one lied ever. I knew that happened, and

I was guilty for stretching the truth. I had lied for John. I had told Maman I wasn't at places when I was. I kept the truth from Maman. But small things.

I wanted to understand the people who I knew, who were the map of me, the foundation of my life. The ones who might have written or erased things, changed the story without me knowing. It was a big thought and it stunned me for just thinking it.

This single thought, a pewter fishing weight downwards, falling in a straight-line through me, my stomach, down past my waist, the inside of my thighs, the drop.

Secrets keep you from people as you keep them.

Stanley was a secret.

I saw him because Mr. Willow's fading mind was letting go of things like a candle gives off heat and spits off water from the wick out. Wasted energy. The candle is used for one thing: light. But the candle gives off the heat and expels the water as well.

I wanted to learn about what happened to John from Mr. Willow. I wanted to know the truth about his looking down a hole. But I didn't get John until right at the end. I got the heat and the spit from the candle, which was Stanley.

But what if Stanley was an answer I should have wanted? Was he the deeper secret that could lead to more answers? He wasn't the right answer for what I was looking.

He still existed in Mr. Willow's memory, that's what I got along with the clock, talking down a hole, in the grate in his room.

Mrs. Bertram knew him, knew of him, knew that name! So he must have been real. Did Pops know him?

She said that she wasn't related to him, why did she say that?

Walking down a hill of knowing nothing. Unpicking all these stitches. I had been threading too many things together, sewing them into the same answer. So I started counting the people around me. Maman, Mrs. Bertram, Pops, Mr. Willow, Bunny, the brothers, looking for ties, to knot things into some sense.

When I got back down to the cottage, its usual warmth and light felt one step removed in me, as if I was at Mr. Willow's window. For all that I wanted it, I couldn't quite let any of it in.

"You okay, Rozel?" called Maman.

"I'm fine Maman," I said, walking upstairs.

"Fifteen minutes til food, darling." Her sing song voice and her soothing way.

Upstairs, in my room, on the table, I wrote in the centre on a piece of paper.

STANLEY.

I circled it then wrote:

POPS, MRS. BERTRAM, MR. WILLOW, JOHN.

In a North, South, East, West formation around the name Stanley.

I had no idea what I was doing but I needed to see all these names down together on a piece of paper.

In the bottom right hand corner I wrote, ROZEL. Then I crossed it out until it was just a block of black.

In the bottom centre I wrote, HOLE.

I stared at it. I heard footsteps coming up the stairs. I quickly folded it and put it into the chimney, on the shelf.

Maman can tell when I worry. She feels it in the air just as I do with her. We sit under the same cloud.

"Rozel, what's going on with you?"

Pops had said he was going out and I had said under my breath "again?" I was angry that he said Jessie instead of Mrs. Bertram. I was thinking how his cow lick looked just like Bunny's. How Bunny never had the words, just like Pops.

Pops was drifting away from me on an undercurrent that Maman did not see or feel.

Maman and Pops equalled one, filling in each other's lacking, working to keep the machinery of daily life ticking over, taking turns to turn the wheel. Pops never spoke about the day I saw him in Mrs. Bertram's kitchen. Pops' words were never the bulk of our interactions, his usual silences were now something I read into. They felt like dark holes to fall into.

"I said, Rozel, what's wrong?" Maman said.

"Why do you never talk to Mrs. Bertram, Maman?"

A question to a question as an answer. Maybe I was more like Mrs. Bertram than I thought.

"We are just not the same sort of people," she said.

"But you are!" I said, louder than I intended.

They held fast with every inch of themselves the people they loved. They were the food, the walls, the chimneys, the fires, both lost but happy in the quiet rituals of their days. They were both the queen of the hive, their skin honeyed by the sun outside.

And they both loved Pops.

Or that was my fear.

"Pops was at her house, they were talking. He knew her first name."

I blurted out, speaking it at the floor. Noticing how the flagstones bulged against the edges of each other, held breaths. They were heavy, too. Was I breaking a bond, a tie and making the family split?

"Is that it, Rozel? Is that why you worry and fidget? Oh, my love. You know I have all the answers, Rozel. Do you think Jessie could stop Pops telling me everything? She could never stop me from knowing anything. See, I even knew there was something wrong with you didn't I? Sit down," she said.

Across the table she brought her arms and clasped my hands and began.

"Bunny doesn't know his dad, but I do. He didn't want to settle, he didn't want to nest. Everything was fine until she got pregnant. His head was lost in the maze of his own frustrations. It sent him crazy. One night Jessie was in the house, up there, and he said he wanted her but not the baby. He hit her! Punched her right in the stomach. Can you imagine being able to do that Rozel? Punch a stomach with a baby inside? His baby? All she did was try and get away from him. You see he lunged for her, lost his footing and his head hit the fireplace, then the stone below." Maman let go of me for a second and banged the table with her fist. The knock of her hand as his skull was shocking. "She looked up and there, at the window, was Mr. Willow. She didn't know why he was there at that moment, she wondered even if he had come to help Bear? Help him get the baby out of her. I can't say really. Who can? I'm putting these thoughts out to fly into the night."

Maman whisked the air with her hand. Then she rested it back down on top of mine to continue talking.

"So, he came in, Mr. Willow. Said he would sort it for her, whatever that meant. She went upstairs in a state. Pops said he came later, to Mrs. Bertram's house, after she had called him. She'd come downstairs to an empty house. The fireplace was wet. It was ormering time." Maman's retelling was jumping around, closing her eyes, to be there, to tell me, even though she was never there. "Bear was gone. Mrs. Bertram had to make sure that everyone thought he had left her. All he had to do, all Pops had to do, was dress in Bear's clothes and take the ferry. That's all your Pops did," she said, shrugging like it was nothing. "Pops told me all of it. Of course he did. You think I wouldn't know, Rozel? We can't hide from each other. I have had his words, his love in my pocket, and he has mine."

Maman had tears resting in the edges of her eyes that didn't fall. She took a deep breath and carried on.

"What's cut Jessie up all these years, everyone calling her Mrs. Bertram. That's the name she would have taken if Bear hadn't left before their wedding. Yes. She carries that name around like it's hers. And the worst of it is she doesn't know if he's dead, if she killed him when she left Mr. Willow to sort it, or if he's alive, or what Mr. Willow did."

She sat back in her chair and her hands pulled back from the top of mine, gave a big sigh and dived back in.

"He was meant to have his dad's name, but she called him Bunny, his dad's nickname was Bear and I guess it put them closer together in her mind. People just think it's short for Brian."

Maman was still talking and as she did she was pulling at the rope and bringing Pops to shore. Away from the horizon and the pulling shallow ormering tide. He'd drifted away from me, out past the shimmering. She was bringing him back to me.

"Mr. Willow leaving that Will all to her, maybe she has to keep his secrets now," Maman said

"But you knew all this?" I said looking at her rosy face.

"No, Rozel, I knew some, and Pops told me all the rest that he knew later, much later. He was shocked when he saw you at her house and he didn't know what you knew. It was when you said Bear's name to Mrs. Bertram. Stanley."

Chapter 40

When I opened my curtains the next morning there was a clean white page of snow with Maman's bleached tea towels, pegged on the line. They were waving their white flags in clapping flaps at the quiet whiter snow.

How white. How quiet. How silently it had crept while we all slept. It was resting on grass blades like the clouds rest above us as we walk. How can thin blades hold such a weight? Is snow a weight? The tree by the gate looks exhausted today. Its shoulders have rolled forward and down with the cold snow blossom holding onto its big limbs. Fistfuls of heavy snow have clumped greedily around the smaller twigs. Everywhere has been touched with the cold, even the corners of the windows have their lightening strikes of frost.

What if the sea had frozen? Can that happen? Can you skate all the way across a sea to a different island? Like the grey silk of a dogfish's skin, a flat shining bridge all the way to the mainland. I went to the small bathroom window opposite my room, unlocked the long cold window arm up off its pin and pushed the window away from me. The cold salty air rushed inwards at me as I looked out on tip toes.

Waves were rolling forward towards the shore with their skirts of white foam. The swirls of a spinning top, forward, coming forward. No, the sea wasn't frozen, it was still alive. Its forward and back looked faster against the soft still down of the snow all around. This small square view was a black and white photograph of my world. All the colours turned off, down to shades. I ran down the stairs and out the back door, without really knowing why I was doing it. I had opened out to an ear cupped silence. I didn't like how the world was quieter out here, more than inside my head. It felt suffocating. Where had all the noise gone? Where was the birdsong? The distant sea was no louder than the rolling waves of my own thoughts. Snow didn't come much to the island and the island seemed unsure of its arrival.

The last time I had seen frost and snow was the day I broke my arm.

I closed my eyes and breathed the cold air in. It smelled of grass and wet towels. Behind my closed eyes, I saw two huge sugar coated crusty eyes open slowly and look at me.

The soldier was still there in my head. He had never left. When a dream comes back to you awake, is it still a dream?

Maman says that anyone you meet in your dreams are really just you dressing up. But I know I am not him.

He is a concrete memory, the hidden steel framework inside the wall. The sharp edges of that day, of him hadn't been smoothed like a pebble with time.

The cemetery on the back hill behind the church had headstones for all the main families on this part of the island. The stone wall that goes all the way around the church, stands without a single name on those stones. The dry-stone wall where every stone no matter its size was used. Pops had told me that was the way to make a stone wall, whatever stone you pick up you have to use otherwise you get tired picking up a stone and putting it down and the wall never gets bigger. That wall, maybe it could be the head stone for my soldier, for all the ones that found themselves washed up here on our tiny island. Where did all the missing ones go? They didn't have a square to rest flowers on, to water with tears.

I always thought it odd that we put people into the ground, then on their birthday cut flowers to place on their graves.

We cut growing things from the ground and rest them on top of the thing we love in the ground!

Maman celebrates with flowers, spring with daffodils trumpeting on the kitchen table. Sometimes Pops will buy her freesias or tulips. He'll hug her and pucker up saying, "Two lips for tulips," and she will laugh and smack him away.

The flowers sit in a jolly conversation of bright colours together, until the water has no more life to give them and they drop themselves petal by petal. The colour drains from then into a paler form or browns but you never see where the colour goes. Where does it go?

The softness of a fallen petal is such a beautiful thing to hold in your hands. If you curl it too hard the wetness from within seeps out and the curl of it becomes a moist grub. I'd squash them in water and try and make perfume in a jam jar, but the smell was mostly of stems and green and none of the beauty of the petals would keep. Maman would dab a little onto her wrists, to make me happy, smell it and say, "Ooh la la."

Each time I thought that this would be the time I would make perfume, exacting the water, choosing the petal.

Today not a single bush was visible, just lumps under the covers.

The snow had covered all the plants.

The garden was only ours because I could see the boundary of the wall make a square of white.

I went back in and put my thicker tights on. I might even cut across the field to save time. Outside the gate, on my walk, all the birds were swooping and swirling looking for food. It was so easy to see the differences. The greens of the chaffinches, the robins like beacons, their red bellies against the snow. A carnival of eager. I must remember to put some food out for them when I come back tonight.

I looked up, marvelling at the little acrobatic dots, so much so I missed my footing and stepped, falling down into a deeper bit of snow.

The comedy of the moment was only mine. I passed Mr. Willow's house with no sign of life. No him at the window. No lights on. The front of the house blank stone and upright with the garden as the grave side. An empty house is always dark, even in the daytime.

I thought of John and his short walk to the Smugglers. His useless leg, dragging like a rudder behind him.

The paths and trails we leave in our wake as we go forward. Drawing our own lines on a page. Today mine would be like an unruly fountain pen snagging and spluttering on the white as I fell forward into the snow watching the birds. John's path would be the dot dash of Morse code as he caught up his good side and his bad leg dragging.

Mrs. Bertram and her bike could be one long line curving elegantly down the cliff.

It was a different world in this white, like it would never go back to the same. That it would be white forever. The salty air from each side of the island usually stopped snow or frost. Rare things are celebrated here like the ormering tide, and everyone was out in it.

The next day it had all but gone, except for the piles that had been made. The snowmen's squat remains, mole-hilled walls scuffed in train lines from path making.

It was as if the snow had never been here. The island had warmed itself back up and sponged, sucking the whole lot of it down into the ground.

This island, this ground of ours that hides the people and grows the flowers.

Washing all our secrets back down for itself.